Seeker One

Voyages of the Seeker #1

By Clint Hollingsworth

Illustration by Clint Hollingsworth

Dedication

To Robert A. Heinlein.

Chapter One

"How did we not know this was all down here? This underground emplacement is huge! "

These were the first words I heard after Krizon put me in the chamber.

I… stasis must be… end…

"The Laldoralin didn't want us to know it was here," a second voice said. "Now that we're operating under what is supposed to be 'full disclosure,' they're telling us where to look."

Can't move… can't see…

"Now that they've supposedly stopped manipulating Earth's path, which even now, I'm not sure is the case. Look at all this tech! And not a spot of dust anywhere."

How long… have we been in stasis? How am I able to think, to be conscious?

"Look, Samuel, we've found the kids. Right where the Laldoralin said they'd be. Looks like the stasis pods activated when we came down here. The reactivation sequence has started. The entire installation is powering up."

"They look human. Somehow, I thought they'd look more…"

"Alien? They supposedly interacted with people every day, back then."

"Note the ears on the boy. He probably had to wear a hoodie, just to go out and about. Can't imagine it was easy being an alien-Terran hybrid."

No! That's supposed to be secret!

"Good-lookin' kids. Half-alien or not."

"Whatever. We're just supposed to get this chamber back to Sci-Admin, and let the 'Dallies' get them outta there. They've been stuck here for a century and a half. I can't even imagine what kind of culture shock these two are about to experience. We've come a long way since the 21st century."

"They're young. They'll adapt."

"Heh. These 'teens' are older than you and I both, combined."

Holy crap. How long have we been down here?

Chapter Two

Nine years later…

Crap. I'm going to be late!

You do not show up late for a summons from an admiral. Cadets don't do that if they want to stay cadets.

"Please people! Make a lane!" I yelled as I moved forward. "Late for a very important date! With Admiral Warren!"

Some of the milling rabble smiled. Since we were at the academy at Terran Exploratory Force headquarters, many of them had dealings with Admiral Warren. They knew damn well the consequences of tardiness. Most were polite enough to get out of the way. I found hall 21-A and was buzzing the admiral's admittance chime a few minutes later.

"Enter, Cadet Voss," the computer's mellow voice said, authorizing me to enter, and I stepped into the massive office of Admiral Indira Wallace. Behind her, through a massive view window, I could see the sagebrush country of the Oregon high desert, one of the few uncrowded regions left on Earth.

I was on time, but the admiral gave me the usual 'you cadets are a blight on the world' expression she uses to such great and intimidating effect.

"Cadet Tanner Voss, reporting as ordered, Admiral." I stood at attention as I said it.

"Cadet." The admiral had a voice like silk and sand paper combined. As she glanced down at her Padd, releasing me from her quantum beam eyes, I realized that her aide, Commander Xiao, was standing behind and to the left of her. Wallace continued, "You've been in the engineering track for the last three and one-half years. Good numbers; you seem competent in that area. What exactly made you choose that field, Mr. Voss?"

"Ma'am?"

"It's a simple question, young man. Why engineering?"

"Well, if you're going to go exploring this part of the spiral arm we exist in, you'd be wise to know how to repair everything you use to get there. And I've always had an affinity for tech. It just seemed like a good fit."

"Yes. Exploring," she said. "You seem to have a real desire to get into space, young man. Tell me why."

What is this all about?

"I want to know," she continued, "more than this comm-screen is telling me. Tell me why you, personally want to go into space."

Oh, I hate these kinds of questions. More like a psychology quiz than any desire to know who I am.

"Why does everyone here at this academy want to go to space? To get off Earth, to go see new things. I want to learn about new worlds, new species. It's a big galaxy, and I want to know what's in it."

"Any particular reason you want 'to get off Earth,' as you put it? Other than the burning desire to see the galaxy?"

"I wouldn't mind going someplace where being the son of a famous alien wasn't such a big deal."

"Ah. I'd guess your last nine years have given you some just cause for that, though hopefully your time here at the academy was not part of that particular difficulty."

"Not at all, ma'am. My fellow cadets and the staff here have been great."

Good. I'm glad to hear it. But, another question; what do you hope for upon graduation, cadet?" The admiral's eyes were half closed as she asked the question over steepled fingers.

"I hope for a berth on a T.E.F. ship, Admiral. To go to other worlds, even if they're worlds already in the Hegemony."

"You are of course aware of the Deep Space Initiative?"

That's an odd question to ask a cadet. Like asking if we know we breathe oxygen.

"Er… yes ma'am, the Big Three. The *Seeker*, the *Searcher*, and the *Wanderer* are all set to head out for space beyond the Hegemony. My sister Valiel is on the…"

"On the *Wanderer*. Yes, I know that, Mr. Voss. The Laldoralin have provided us with the opportunity to explore areas beyond their known star charts using our own variant of their translocation drive technology." The admiral glanced down at her personal CommPadd. "And since the very existence of this academy is founded on training people like yourself to join the Terran Exploration Force, you might be interested to know that you are being transferred to the *E.E.S. Seeker,* immediately."

What?

"Ma'am, you are aware that I still have a full year to go before I graduate, are you not?" As I looked at her, Commander Xiao left her side and walked around behind me and stood in the corner to my right. I could feel him there…. and something felt odd.

"I am well aware of every facet of your life, cadet. You have made amazing progress for someone born over one hundred and sixty years ago."

There it was. My history once again intruding into my current life. Being one hundred and sixty-four years old really doesn't mean much if you spent one hundred and forty of those years in a Laldoralin stasis chamber, basically abandoned when the experiment was deemed finished.

"So… this is regarding my… hybrid status then?"

"It has a bearing. Myself, I would prefer our students finish their studies here at the academy, where mistakes have a low-price threshold, rather than in deep space where mistakes can be fatal. However, I have been overruled by your father."

That was perplexing. "I can't imagine that Ronald Voss, the textbook absent-minded professor, would try to…"

"Not your guardian, Tanner. Your sire. Your real father."

Krizon.

For a moment, I couldn't speak, could barely process what I was hearing. I felt my resentment rise, like a geyser I had no control valve on. My Laldoralin 'sperm donor,' my handler, the one who had imprisoned me when I was no longer needed, I'd never be calling him father. He had overseen my training back in 21st century Earth, coached me in a number of disciplines, but he was never fatherly. Valiel and I had always felt like a lab rats around the Laldoralin's lead administrator for the 'Earth Project.'

"I… see," I said. "I greatly appreciate this opportunity, Admiral, and I wholeheartedly wish to accept it, but please understand my confusion. I quite literally have not heard from that particular sentient in over a century and a half. Needless to say, I'm surprised to learn he's taken an interest in my life now."

"Krizon is important in both Terran and 'Doralin circles. He's a preeminent scientist to his people, and the architect of Earth's entrance into the stellar community. Being his son is nothing to be upset about," she said, a slightly disdainful expression on her face.

"Krizon has numerous offspring, Admiral. Many of them cross-pollinated with other humanoid species." I made sure not to let emotion color my response, but it wasn't easy.

Tamp it down, man. This is an admiral you're talking to. She can break you and have you expelled at a moment's notice.

"True, Mr. Voss. But none of those other hybrids, that we know of, have your, and of course your sister's… interesting talents. Talents that are a reflection of your mixed heritage. Talents that have not shown up in most other hybrid children, I might add."

So that's what this is about. The old devil wants to make sure we don't waste what we've wound up with as a result of our genetic mulligan stew.

It was then I felt the threat. Before I even consciously registered what was happening, I dodged my head four inches to the left, just as a small red rubber ball went whizzing by where my head had been. The admiral watched as the ball bounced off the corner of her office. She looked at me, I looked over my shoulder at Xiao. The commander simply stood impassively, at parade rest.

"A test, ma'am?" I asked.

"Indeed, Cadet. Here's another." She took a similar ball, blue this time, from her desk, and tossed it to me. "Commander Xiao's CommPadd is on his belt. Hit it with this."

I started to turn, intending to lob it at Xiao.

"Without looking or turning, please," she said.

Of course, we want to see the freak in action.

He didn't make a sound, but I felt Xiao change position. I flipped the ball back over my right shoulder and I knew it was on target before it left my hand. A second later I heard it hit the small device.

The admiral smiled for the first time, possibly ever.

"My records show that your marks in combat training were not only off the charts, but Commander Donohue mentions in your records that your ability to hit your targets was impossibly, ridiculously accurate. He also said you were almost impossible to ambush. A sixth sense, I presume?"

"I suppose so, ma'am…"

"Six months ago, those stats took a nosedive for some reason," she said, looking up from her Padd. She managed to look both questioning and disdainful in one expression, and impressive ability in itself. "Have you ever heard the term 'sandbagging,' cadet?"

"To prevent flooding?" I knew damn well what she was talking about, but I didn't want to admit I'd not been giving my all, trying to lessen my freak-hybrid status. The admiral just stared at me, the silence extending into the very uncomfortable range.

"Ah, perhaps you mean the practice of purposely underperforming?" I asked.

"That would be the meaning I'm referring to. I remind you that evasion does not become an Exploratory Force officer."

I sighed. "Yes, Admiral, I… perhaps did not give 100 percent on my later sims. I was starting to get some… comments from my fellow cadets. I dropped my scores just enough not to stand out anymore. As a hybrid, I guess I'm a little sensitive to discussions of my partial Terran status."

"So, you made sure to fall to the level of the people around you. I see."

"Ma'am, we're, as you said, an explorer group. I'm not even sure why we need to have all this military-style training. I just thought I should concentrate on the sciences needed to run the ship and gather data."

The ol' gal looked at me, her expression now enigmatic, seeming to weigh her words carefully.

"Cadet. I am about to impart information to you that only graduates of this institution are privy to. It is not for public consumption.

You are not to speak of it to anyone who is not T.E.F. personnel. Do you understand this, and swear to keep this information private?"

"Yes ma'am. I so swear."

This was evidently not the usual scuttlebutt that runs through institutions of higher learning. My guess was the whole "Let's journey to the stars" drive Earth had been on since the Laldoralin announced themselves was missing some important info. I was right.

"Since our extra-terrestrial allies first began helping us get up to intergalactic speed, we've been kept abreast of what's going on in our little corner of the galaxy. As huge as it is, the Laldoralin-led Alliance of Systems, The Hegemony, only covers a tiny fraction of galactic space. We are on one lonely little arm of the spiral, and even with the areas explored by the races 'senior' to us, there is an incredible amount of territory that hasn't been explored. Never been examined by the races we know of."

Nothing new about that, but I could sense she had something a bit heavier to impart.

"What is not public knowledge, cadet, is that along with the eleven friendly races in the Laldoralin Hegemony, there are some rather unfriendly races, races who prey on their neighbors. Earth is fortunate that most of those races are on the other side of Laldoralin space, but there are two: the ZiSar and the Klugg, which we've only been spared meeting due to the efforts of the Alliance of Systems. You will have time and opportunity to learn about these races once aboard the *Seeker*. I assure you, the knowledge will be chilling."

"If I may ask, why has this been kept under wraps, ma'am?"

"What is the biggest problem our world faces, Voss? Even now, when we've come so far in undoing the problems of the previous century?"

"I'd guess," I said, scrambling in the face of her question to my question, "it's still overpopulation."

"Indeed. We, as a species, are crowding the other species and the natural resources of Earth to the edge. There are simply too many people on this planet, and after two centuries, there are still no political leaders with enough spine to push for mitigating the problem with scientific means. Last century, while you 'slept,' wars started to break out over this problem. The only reason we're still here is due to the private efforts of groups who have managed to get free birth control into the hands of ninety percent of the world's women."

"So, I guess that's the reason for the push for galactic exploration."

"It is. The people of Earth need a reason to be pioneers again. The Terran Exploration Force is going to give them that reason by finding new, unclaimed worlds and starting colonies there. But, if word gets out that dangerous groups of hostile races stack the deck in any way against survival, we think the whole movement might stall. We cannot afford for that to happen. We're already getting dangerous pushback from extremist groups, like the Earth For Earth movement."

I saw the problem. With the help of our alien visitors, we were mining the solar system, colonizing Mars and trading with races across the Hegemony. But it had gotten to the point where all the beautiful places on Earth had waiting lists and finding a place to breath the fresh air and smell the trees without a lot of prior planning was more and more difficult. One of our presidents in the late 21st century had even tried to sell the National Parks for development so he and his cronies could profit. Fortunately, he'd been thwarted.

The problem hadn't been half as bad in the mid-21st century, but the seeds of the problem had been in place even then. The amount of development that had arisen to service an exponentially growing population had horrified me when we'd been "unthawed." Giving people the chance to move out in the galaxy was the best solution for Earth and its people.

"This threat of alien hostility is why you are shipping out on the *Seeker*, Cadet. You will be tutored by experienced officers onboard and you'll be able to continue learning in your engineering track: however, you will also be in the duty rotation for ship's defense. You will be the Junior Tactical officer." The Admiral gave me a slight, sad smile. "I know this is a lot on your shoulders young man, but the stakes are high."

"Yes, Admiral. Ready to do my part."

"Good. You ship out on the New Phoenix Shuttle at 13:00 tomorrow. Have your affairs in order before then," she said. "Good luck, Cadet. Dismissed."

And my life was changed with those parting words.

Chapter Three

"You're shipping out on the *Seeker?* For space? But you haven't even graduated!"

"Y'know, Deena, that is exactly what I told the admiral. She said 'Shaddup and pack.'"

My pal and lab partner in Translocation Astrophysics, Deena was a short, curvy young cadet from the U.K. She was also my tutor in the civilized game of draw poker. Her lessons were pretty expensive, though eventually I began to lessen the expense and amortize the cost by learning to see her tells when she was bluffing. Her poker face became unconsciously crafty if you knew what to look for.

"This has to do with your thing, doesn't it?"

"Why, Deena! Such unseemly conversation for a future officer."

"Not that thing, you wanker. I mean why we call you Sure Shot."

"Actually, Deeners," I said, somewhat regretfully, "that would fall under classified."

"This from the man no one in this entire school will gamble with on a game of darts. What's so important that they'd pull you early like this? A whole year early?"

I debated how much to say. Deena was a good friend, one of the best, and I didn't have that many. When she latched onto a question or problem, though, she was like a British bulldog. She'd make a great science officer someday.

"The *Seeker* is not going to be exploring inside the Hegemony, we know that." She looked at me for a moment, and I could see the program running in her head. "They're going out into the dark regions. Beyond where the Dallies have explored."

"Actually, maybe I've said too much already."

"Let's see now. You're a reasonably good engineer, but not the best in our class, so it must have to do with your fancy gift. From all the stuff they've been training us on, the combat and ship to ship sims…" She looked at me, alarmed. "They're expectin' trouble out there!"

"Nothing definite. I guess the brass just wants to hedge their bets." I didn't mention Krizon's mechanizations; there were some things I didn't need to share. I found in my heart that having my estranged father manipulating events was embarrassing. Like I would have to prove that I actually had some merit beyond having an influential 'parent.' I was already imagining I was going to get crap about that.

"So, I finish my schooling on the ship," I said. "Eat your heart out, cadet!"

I expected a snappy comeback. What I got was a hug, and big solemn eyes looking deeply into mine.

"Tanner," she said, "try not to die out there. Okay?"

"Ah… all right. I'll do m' best. Deena, don't worry. Everything will be fine. I wish you could go to."

"You an' me both," she said, "but don't cha worry. I'll be right behind you on the next wave, to fix your flub-ups."

The rest of that day was spent contacting the people I knew and letting them know I was going to be incommunicado. I'm not the most gregarious person you'll find, but I've managed to make a few friends over the years who are real ones. They were people who've been able to get past the pointed ears, the angled eyebrows, aqua eyes, and the slightly metallic sheen of my brown/bronze skin. Most of them expressed happiness for me that I was going to space a year early.

However, my foster dad was not one to do so. Ronald Voss was usually over the moon and very supportive when I achieved something, but this was not one of those times.

"They're sending you out a year before you graduate? Where exactly are you going, son?" His tanned face and white beard glowered at me out of my CommPadd.

"Can't say exactly, Ron, but it is aboard the *Seeker*, so you know it's going to be new. I haven't seen the mission briefs. All I can tell you is that tomorrow I am to be aboard ship and ready to go," I told him. "I just wanted to make sure you knew where I was going. I tried to call Valiel, but she seems to have gone comm-silent."

"Your sister was recalled to her ship, and wouldn't share the reason with me. She's always been closed-mouthed about things. If I know how things work, these two sudden changes in your lives cannot be coincidence. This is too soon. I didn't think those vessels were ready to leave, and I sure never expected that both my kids would be on them."

This may sound odd, but hearing the upset in my foster father's voice actually gave me a slightly warm feeling in my chest. Not because he was upset, but because I knew he *really* did care about Val and I. My sister and I both had some issues around abandonment.

Even our "fake" mother and father, Evan and Dora Kincaid, people that Krizon had co-opted into taking care of us back then, had been a million times more warm than the 'alien in the basement' who was our real father. We still had issues around Evan and Dora, having woke up in a future in which they were long dead.

There are people who never have any parents, so, in one sense, Val and I hit the jackpot. Ronald Voss was our third parent out of four—three out of those four being *good* parents. But, in another sense, it messed with our minds. Not that my foster father wasn't important—far from it—but our personalities were already set when we met him. For this reason, I always called my step-Dad "Ron," not "Dad," and he didn't seem to mind.

The first few years out of stasis had been pretty overwhelming. Imagine, if you can, everyone you know gone, every concept you believed changed. Val had dealt with it by becoming closed off.

My method had been to get into trouble on a regular basis. If Ronald Voss hadn't been the paradigm for kindness and patience, I doubt Val and I would have done as well as we had. Hell, I might've wound up in jail, which was definitely still a thing in this century.

For the moment though, my foster father's face became suspicious as he looked out of the comm-screen at me. "I sense some Laldoralin meddling here."

"It's… ah… Krizon." There was no point in not telling him.

"Of course it is," he said, his voice dripping with bitterness. "It wasn't bad enough that he…"

"Ron, please. Let's not go through it again. You've been more of a father in nine years than he was in a century and a half, but rehashing it doesn't help me, or Val. Bottom line is, I'm shipping out, and I think it's going to be a great opportunity, learning on the job. So, be happy for me. I'm stoked."

"Stoked. I will miss those archaic terms you always use. All right," He looked off screen for a moment and his sad expression tore at my heart. "Remember all I taught you: be aware, have your Get Home Bag ready, and learn everything you can. And for God's sake, be sure to come back in one piece."

"I will, and I can't see that I'll be using a Get Home Bag in deep space, not many places to evac there."

"It's light, so humor me. Besides, most of those ships have escape pods, right? Well, your little bag might be handy if you ever need to get off your vessel."

"Sure, I'll take it," I said. "Aside from uniforms and my ReadPadd, I'm not taking much else, so I'm sure it'll fit within my allotment. Do you mind if I ship the rest of my stuff to you for storage?"

"This is your home, Tanner. You are always welcome here, and I'll be glad to put your things in your room."

"What? You haven't rented it out already?"

"Not 'til next Tuesday," he said with a dry tone. "Good luck, son. May you always find your way back."

"Goodbye, Ron… uh… Dad."

I signed off, and felt a deep ache in my chest. I would miss him. The people who are your true family are the ones who are there for you. Genetics, on the other hand, is just the luck of the draw.

Chapter Four

I was almost at my destination, the Hyperloop Rail link in Portland, having taken a rental self-driver from the civilian contract agency at T.E.F. headquarters. Self-drivers had been in their infancy before I was put in stasis, but riding in one alone across the state gave me a little too much time to think. I was still a little freaked out.

It wasn't just having my life uprooted, because I was excited to get a berth on the *Seeker*, one of the Big Three, the deep space explorers. It was also the admiral's latter comments on the dangerous races in our own neighborhood.

That came as a bit of a shocker. I wouldn't say the information scared me, but it certainly didn't put my mind at ease.

I understood why the Laldoralin had kept this information on the Q.T., considering some of the crazed reactions when they, a peaceful alien race, had made their presence known. Humanity, *en masse,* learning about other extremely hostile races nearby, would have sent a certain contingent of the human race into dangerous panic.

And humans were never more dangerous than when they were afraid.

The T.E.F. academy is in the middle of the Oregon deserts, east of the Cascade mountain chain, but the hyper loop rail system didn't go there. To get a ride to New Phoenix, I had to go to Portland, along the old I-5 corridor.

I had been to Portland a number of times when I was a kid. My parents, Evan and Dora, drove Val and me to the big city once a month to get supplies for our semi-coastal home (which covered Krizon's subterranean emplacement).

Portland had changed. Most of the elegant older buildings had gone the way of the dodo, unless they were of great historical significance. The once-busy streets now only had occasional traffic from self-driving transit vehicles, though, occasionally, antique specially licensed human-driven cars could be seen.

As I neared the station, my gut began to clench, a sure sign of trouble.

I had taken a single-pod self-driver unit from the academy to the center of station, where I would cut it loose to return to the nearest vending garage. I was about two blocks from the hyper-rail embarkation station when I realized something was amiss. The car wasn't dropping me off at the right place.

It stubbornly insisted that I exit the vehicle, and realizing the futility of arguing with a programmed computer, I got out. I pulled my hat out of my duffel and pulled it down over my ears, and put on my sunglasses.

I realized there was a parade coming down the street toward me.

No, not a parade, a protest.

I have no problem with people peacefully protesting over their current opinionated point of view, none at all. Unless, of course, they're anti-alien whack jobs who've made it necessary for my entire family to be on alert while for the last nine years.

And… the universe decreed they were that kind of protesters. Earth For Earth signs all over the place, and they were walking right toward me.

Oh. Shit.

My cadet hat, with the droppable ear flaps, covered my ears, and my dark glasses covered my aqua eyes, but the entire group seemed to be centering its attention on me. I turned and tried to backtrack toward the street I'd just come down, but my deep blue cadet uniform stood out like a sore thumb and drew the attention of the crowd.

These jerks were known for harassing any space-related professionals, but they had a particular dislike for T.E.F. personnel. And one Einstein in the crowd called me out.

"It's him!" the guy yelled. "It's the hybrid devil boy!"

Hybrid devil boy? Are you kidding me?

Celebrity status can really suck. Every eye in the crowed followed me, eyes starting to fill with righteous fury.

"Oh, crap." I said, ducking my head and picking up speed. My heart began pounding and I heard that sound. The sound of many people starting to move as a group, in my direction, their pace breaking into a run.

I kicked in the turbos and began sprinting. Cadets aren't armed. It doesn't look good on a person's resumé to be using a beamer on a crowd of protesters, no matter how tempting. In this case, escape was the best defense. I had a sneaking suspicion these jack holes had been waiting for me, and I prayed they hadn't been so organized as to cut off every escape route.

I have a few little advantages over the average human. My hybrid genes give me a little extra strength and I used that to try and distance myself from them, but I couldn't outrun the rocks they were throwing. I felt something about to impact with my head, and jerked it sideways, just missing a knock to the skull. This set me off balance, and at the speed I was moving, I began to lose my balance. The final straw was a box that someone had stupidly tossed out the back door of their shop.

Crashed and burned.

A woman caught up to me first, and grabbed at my duffel. If you've ever thought about how certain people resemble their pets, hers must have been a particularly bad-tempered Doberman. The others were right behind her, and I decided this wasn't a time to be worried about quaint notions of chivalry. I spun, forcing her to spin with me. She came around, tripped over the same box I had and went sprawling.

The group cry of outrage behind us was chilling.

I tried to turn to flee again, but a large man with a sign swung it at me, and I had to swing my duffel to block it. I snapped a hard kick into his belly and for a moment, fate was on my side. His large body fell right at the feet of the first wave of the crowd, bringing down several, and causing, what under other circumstance would have been a comedic human traffic jam.

If I'd had an FTL drive, I would have used it, but being a bio sentient, I gave the best imitation of 'Faster Than Light' that my legs would provide. If I could get far enough ahead, I could comm the local police. It being early, there was hardly anyone else on the street, and no one to help me. If I could find a surveillance cam, maybe the police might come. But there was no guarantee they'd come in time to be of any help.

I knew, in some way that probably was an off-shoot of my danger sense, where the hyper loop station was, even though I couldn't see it. I also knew I needed to be on the train in the next five minutes, or it would be an hour until the next one.

I didn't really care to spend an hour in this area. I don't want to admit I was terrified, but… yeah. I don't want to admit that.

I'd sprinted far enough ahead of the crowd that I was able to turn a corner and be out of their sight, and I went into the first door I came to, fortunately unlocked. As soon as I was through the door frame, I turned and clicked the deadbolt, locking the door behind me. My heart was hammering with near panic.

"Hey man, you're not supposed to be in here." I turned to see a man of middle years, whose ancestors at one time had come from Asia. He did not seem pleased to see someone in his kitchen who wasn't there to cook. He took in my uniform and his expression changed.

"Hey! You're T.E.F., aren't you? That's mega!"

"Just a cadet, at this point. I'm sorry to barge in, but there's a bunch of anti-alien protesters out there that want my blood. I'm just trying to get to the hyper loop station."

"Son of a…" He noticed my ears, took in my aqua eyes, and shook his head. "C'mon, there's a side door on the other end of the kitchen. I can step out first to make sure they've gone past. The 'Loop' is only two blocks south."

"Oh, that would awesome."

"Awesome? There's a term I haven't heard in years." He opened the second door and stepped out. I watched from inside as he went from one end of the alley to the other. Coming back to the door, he told me, "They're all out front, now. Go right here, and then cross over to that alley. Zoom down that, take a left on the next street, and a right into the alley on the far side. That'll put you almost on top of the station."

"Thank you. You are literally saving my life."

"Anything for our intrepid explorers. Maybe you'll find more intelligent life out there than you've found here."

I gave him a thumbs up and took off down the alley.

Chapter Five

I hate those bastards.

Sitting on the train, fuming, I would have gladly pushed a button that would've vaporized every Earth For Earth member in the world, without hesitation. They'd made my life a "constantly looking over my shoulder" living hell almost from the time Val and I had first made the news when we were rescued. I did my best to calm my mind, but it wasn't easy.

I took a moment to comm the academy, asking for the security office. The academy is attached to the main HQ for the Terran Exploratory Force, and the security personnel there are top notch people. I hoped they'd take me seriously.

After being put through, I was routed to a lieutenant, wearing the security uniform that even the lowliest freshman cadet recognized.

"Hello, Cadet Voss, I'm Lt. Vasquez. What is this concerning?"

"Hello, sir," I replied. "I am assuming that you are looking at a screen with my records?"

"Standard procedure, Mr. Voss."

"Then you probably are now aware of my history, and my troubles with the Earth For Earth people?"

"I am."

"I have been assigned to meet a shuttle in New Phoenix, and I took a self-driver to Portland to catch the Link. Lieutenant, when I reached Portland, my vehicle, rather than dropping me at the station, dropped me off a few blocks away. When I arrived, there was a large group of E.F.E. people there, and they recognized me before I was even all the way out of the car. Like they were waiting for me to arrive."

Vasquez stared at me through the comm screen for a moment.

"So, you are saying, if I am hearing this right, that someone at the car rental office tipped these dirtbags off, and hand delivered you into their grasp?"

"Sir, I don't see any other way to read this."

Vasquez face darkened.

"As you know, the car agency is a civilian contractor. Though we try to vet everyone that is on these grounds, the vetting for civilians is sometimes more problematic than we'd like. Mr. Voss, I will be opening an investigation into this. If I find one of these people has purposefully endangered one of our personnel, they are not going to like the direction of their life from that point on. If they set you up, I promise you, Cadet, I *will* find them."

"Thank you, Lieutenant."

"How can I contact you if I have questions?"

"The Admiral is sending me off-world, sir. I am not sure when I'll be back."

"Understood. Be cautious, young man. Vasquez out."

I hoped he'd find whoever had put me in danger, But not just for me. Having agents of the militant arm of Earth For Earth in the area of our headquarters and our academy could be dangerous to everyone.

I arrived at New Phoenix in a relatively short time, having eventually regained my composure after the events in Portland.

When I was put in storage in the mid-21st century, that train run would have taken at least a couple days. Today, I was in Arizona in well under two hours. I was at the New Phoenix shuttle pad almost a full hour before liftoff, actually beating the pilot by twenty minutes. I could have taken a little time to see the city, but after my send-off earlier, I preferred to sit within the security of an Exploratory Force compound.

Sitting on the ground and leaning on a bench with my small duffel and my backpack, I could look out over the desert landscape of New Phoenix, a city that hadn't existed one hundred and fifty years ago.

Around fifty years into my long sleep, there had been a terrorist attack by another strange group known as the Life Reduction

Front, a bunch of population control fanatics that actually thought detonating a suitcase nuke in a heavily populated Arizona city was going to help the environment. They definitely managed to reduce the population in Arizona for a time, as well as making the original city of Phoenix unlivable. They also were hunted down and executed, but I guess for homicidal nut jobs, that's a small price to pay.

Earth had made some efforts, mostly after the announcement that we weren't alone in the universe, to control its population growth. Mostly this came in the form of colonizing Mars, but we were still a crowded people. I could look out towards what had been empty desert a century ago and see housing developments still sprouting like mushrooms, water pumped in from desalination plants on the Pacific Ocean.

It made me feel a bit sick. My dad, my sister, and I had done camping and survival training out there, but now there were housing developments on a good portion of the lands we'd wandered.

Some countries had made birth control freely available; others had found the very notion to be a blasphemy against their religion. It shouldn't come as shock to anyone that the latter had more immigrants trying to get into the former, than the reverse. In the end, the planet was under the weight of twelve billion pairs of human feet. It could have been worse, and it was even getting better with dropping birthrates, but we needed to find places to move to or it was going to be a long time before the problem was fixed.

In twenty years, the Mars terraforming project would be finished, and migration could start. If the Deep Space Initiative found new worlds already habitable, and had enough adventurous souls willing to try something new, that would reduce the strain on Earth… maybe all the developed landscape out there could be returned to its natural state. At least I sure hoped so. Earth deserved better than to be a human anthill.

Hey, maybe all the Earth For Earth members could be moved to the farthest colony, and we could conveniently forget that it existed.

"Are you my package, Cadet?"

Broken out of my thoughts, I looked up to see a compact man with dark, slicked-back hair, a T.E.F. uniform, and a pilot's clip emblem on his sleeve.

"Yes, Lieutenant, I guess I'm a bit early. No one else seems to have shown up yet."

"Won't be anyone else. Taking you solo on this one. You are, if I'm not mistaken, the last crew member to board the *Seeker*. A last minute-addition?"

"I guess so," I told him. "I only found out I was going yesterday afternoon."

"Interesting," he said, somewhat wistfully. "Wish I was deep spacin', too. Flyin' a shuttle isn't exactly what I was hoping to do with my career. But, maybe someday. I'm gonna do my preflight, then you can board."

"I saw the flight mechanics doing the preflight about ten minutes ago."

"Cadet, a little wisdom to take with you," he said, winking. "As long as you have time, always do your own checking. The ground crew aren't the ones who crash if something goes wrong."

"Point taken." I sat back down on the bench and waited.

Ten minutes later, the side door opened and he pointed at me then gave the thumbs up. I slung my duffel and grabbed my pack by the haul strap and walked in. There were eight seats in the back section, but seeing that the pilot was the only other person on the boat, I looked meaningfully at the co-pilot seat. He nodded. I stowed my gear in a small rack behind the seat, and sat next to him.

He was smooth. The shuttle anti-gravved off its pad with nothing resembling a wobble, and when we hit approximately thirty feet up, he engaged his magnetic propulsion system.

"New Phoenix Traffic Control, this is shuttle *Monte Cristo*. We are lifting and following flight plan 5242. En route to orbital platform Ticonderoga."

"This is Traffic Control. You are green on our boards, *Monte Cristo*. Happy trails."

Rising up through traffic, we eventually hit the upper lanes and continued southwest, toward the Pacific. We could see a huge storm coming in from the ocean. Shot through with lightning, it looked like the wrath of God, but it was going to be a windfall for parched southern California and Baja. We hit our egress point, left the atmosphere, and ventured out into an ocean of a different kind. A vast black endless ocean full of stars, most of which you couldn't see planetside.

The same magnetic system that propelled the shuttle also provided gravity within the cabin, which I was grateful for. Weightlessness didn't make me ill when I'd been in training, but there were a few "acid reflux" moments.

Not everyone was so lucky, though. On our first training run in an orbital sim ship, a few cadets had painted the walls, as well as everyone else.

"Hey, there's New Zealand!" I said. "That's where my dad lives."

"Maybe you can see your house from here," the lieutenant said, smiling. "We're coming around equatorial quadrant seven, Ticonderoga is just coming into view, and your ride is moored just a few miles from her. If you put on your TeeGeeVee, you can see her."

I pulled my TechGogglesVisor out of my duffel, and put them on. The visor interacted with the orbital network and in a few moments, all the objects in our path began to have highlights and info drop-downs in front of my eyes.

Turning my head in small movements, I was able to sort through the myriad of craft, satellites and platforms until I picked out Ticonderoga Platform. I verbally commanded the visor to isolate the station and all nearby vessels and all the other items faded to transparency. The enhanced image showed the station, and beyond her, a large sleek ship in a mooring dock. The *Seeker*.

"That's damn impressive," I said.

"You're a master of understatement, Cadet."

She was two thousand, one hundred and eight feet long, with a flattened tubular hull that seemed vaguely dolphin-like. Adding to that illusion was the flying command bridge that extended from the central hull. The bridge could be retracted during cosmic storms or other unpleasantries. Having your command section sticking out from the ship seemed a little extravagant, but it sure made the ship seem majestic.

Actually, I also thought the extended bridge and the rear jump foils made the stellar vessel look vaguely like a cross between an ancient bi-plane and a submarine, but who was I to argue with the designers? The three explorer ships were all the same design.

I wonder what Val thought when she first saw the Wanderer?

The aft section held the jump foils, two flattened arcs that extended from the ship; one on top, one on bottom. The bottom foil sat slightly more forward on the hull than the top one. These were the jump emitters that helped the ship open a portal into Nth space.

The forward section was shaped like a rounded arrowhead, the hull widening where it started. I had been sent the ship's specifications via my CommPadd the night before, and had been reading up on her every chance I had. The forward hull was the info gathering area. It's where all the sensor gear and the Remora mobile AIs were housed.

I still had a lot more reading to do about my new home.

"*Seeker*, this is shuttle *Monte Cristo* with personnel transfer. Requesting attachment vector," the pilot said.

"Acknowledged *Monte Cristo*. Please stand by," our comm speaker replied.

"Attachment? We're going to latch on?" I asked him.

"Yeah. The *Seeker's* landing craft bay is full at the moment with LCs and Scoot Pods for EVA work. They've got a nice hatch for us, only a slight grav-shift when you board her."

"*Seeker* to *Monte Cristo*," the comm said. "Hold position at these coordinates for temporary rendezvous."

"Er…" the pilot replied. "Rendezvous with whom, *Seeker*?"

"Hold position at attached coordinates, *Monte Cristo*, and await further instructions."

"Acknowledged. *Monte Cristo* out."

"Well," I said. "That was nicely cryptic."

"My guess is that with you being my only cargo, it has something to do with you."

Somehow, that didn't make me feel any less apprehensive. The pilot moved forward and sunward for about five minutes, then brought our craft to a halt.

"Well," he said, "here we are. Guess we'll have to… HOLY CRAP!!"

My heart jumped into my throat as the *Seeker* and Ticonderoga platform were suddenly blotted out by a shape that took up our entire viewing area. Terran ships were required to be at least half a million miles distant from any planet before moving into faster than light (FTL) speed.

From the shape of the huge ship in front of us, that restriction didn't apply to Laldoralin vessels.

Chapter Six

"Earth shuttle," a pleasant female voice spoke from our comm, "this is the *LV Kaialai*, please release your craft to our auto-navigation system."

"Acknowledged. Navigation controls are yours, *Kaialai*." The pilot looked at me, as if to say, '*What have you gotten me into?*'

Hell if I knew.

We began to move toward the ship and a large vented hatch irised open. The hanger bay we entered was like the main hanger at the academy, almost cavernous. We drifted in past some smaller Dallie vessels, coming to an inertia-less landing on a pad near the back.

A Laldoralin woman in a long, almost floor-length uniform coat, awaited us serenely as we debarked the shuttle. Like all the Dallies, her dark, coppery skin was flawless, her high eyebrows pointing up at a thirty degree angle, and her pupil-less aqua colored eyes regarded us with no detectable emotion. She stood a good five or so inches taller than my six-foot-five, and she towered over my more compact companion.

"Greetings. I am Prime Shipboard Commander Kapyoin. What your rank system would call… captain of this vessel. Pilot Nguyen, refreshments have been prepared for you in the lounge just outside our shuttle bay," she said in a mellifluous voice. "Through that door, and through the right. Earthfeed video is available for your entertainment."

"Thanks," Nguyen said. "Seems like this might be a good time to take a meditation break."

"An excellent choice of activities." She turned and headed for a different door at the end of the bay. "Tanner Voss, will you please accompany me?"

"Keep the engine running," I said to Nguyen. "Just in case I break the good china by accident."

The pilot grinned, gave me a thumbs up and headed toward the lounge. I turned and followed my host out of the hanger.

"Are you well, Tanner Voss?" she asked. The Laldoralin try to make small talk, to make Terrans feel more comfortable. They're really not very good at it, but they do make the effort.

"I'm fine, thank you for asking, Prime Commander," I replied. "It is a great honor that you would personally greet someone from one of the younger worlds, particularly a cadet."

She turned to me, with what could be best described as a perplexed look, something I was not accustomed to from her species. The Laldoralin that I had met on Earth since being 'thawed' had always acted like they knew everything in the universe.

"Is it possible that you do not know who you are, Tanner Voss?"

"I think... I do." I replied, but the question had thrown me a little. There were more than a few unanswered questions in my past. "What do you mean? Commander? I am the son of Krizon, half Laldorian and half human. I am a cadet in the Terran Exploratory Force. I have one sister, Valiel, and no other living relatives that I know of. I'm not sure what you refer to."

"Then you know and you don't know. These things are not for me to discuss. Our leader will tell you what you need to know." She turned and continued up the corridor.

The captain is the head honcho on almost any vessel, and that goes for the Laldoralin fleet as well. It was possible there could be a version of a commodore aboard, but I had a sneaking suspicion who the leader here was, simply because of my current situation.

We came to a large, open, austere conference room with a tall figure standing at a large viewport, looking out over the Earth. I recognized him at once, and felt an unexpected rush of resentment that I had to work to contain.

"Hello Father. Long time no see. Long. Time."

Krizon turned toward me, then to the captain, and said something in his calm, mellow voice in Lallanyr, the Dallie language. Captain Kapyoin bowed and left.

"You appear well, my son."

"I am surprised you would have any memory of how I look, after so much time."

"Ah. You are resentful of having been placed in stasis, I see."

"Not at all. I'm resentful of being *left* in stasis. For over a hundred and fifty years. I went to sleep, and everyone I had known and cared about was dead. It sort of soured me on your familial concern," I said, a growing heat building in my chest. "Even Dora and Evan, the people you enlisted to be my above-ground parents… who, by the way, were far better at being there for me than you ever were… are gone, and I didn't even have a chance to say goodbye."

"If you wish, I can bring them to you. Their programs are still active, and re-fabricating their frames would be a simple matter."

"They even… they… what?"

"During our time shepherding Earth, we have used androids on numerous occasions. Dora and Evan were extremely advanced AIs due to the long-term nature of their assignments. Both of them are non-corporeal members of this crew. Would you like to speak to them? They were quite excited that you would be coming aboard."

I felt my knees go weak, a condition I thought was just a figure of speech before this. I sat down on one of the sofas that ringed the circular room, feeling dizzy.

"W-what? You're telling me that the people who actually raised me, who kept my childhood from being one unending science experiment, you're saying they weren't real?"

"They were quite real, Tanner," Krizon said, mild reproach in his voice. "They are simply not biological beings. They are beings who are some of the most advanced AIs you will find in the known galaxy. To make such a statement is somewhat discriminatory, my son."

"They were a lie," I said, barely able to keep my voice from becoming strident. "Like most of what passed for my childhood."

Krizon turned back to the port. Even from the side, I could see he had a pained expression on his face, a mild emotional reaction. That was something not often seen in a Laldoralin.

"Who, then, was my real mother?" I said, scrambling for some emotional control.

"Her name was Sarabeth Williams. She was an astronaut in your pre-emergence space program, a brilliant scientist, an athlete with a stunningly excellent genetic profile. She also had donated some of her ovum to a facility that she might have children after her mission, being concerned that the radiation she might be exposed to might damage her ability to produce offspring. You may have read about that unfortunate spaceflight, the Mars mission on the first inter-system vessel *Eagle*."

"The one that crashed on Mars in 2041."

"Yes. I am pleased her genetic line was not lost, in fact producing offspring which far exceeded our expectations. Tanner, it is because of you and your sister that Earth was included in our hybridization project, and was thus introduced into galactic society centuries before its people might have otherwise been."

How do you respond to that?

"What does that mean, exactly?" I asked.

"We monitored Earth for several centuries before we were forced to become involved at the time of your beginning nuclear age. Humanity has almost destroyed itself in more than one way at more than one time."

"When they weren't getting closed to nuclear annihilation, they refused to take action against human-generated environmental change, which was causing oceanic encroachment upon their shorelines, swallowing whole cities, and killing hundreds of thousands with extreme weather patterns. Planetary overpopulation had reached extreme numbers, and yet the many factions did not support free birth control."

"And the Laldoralin sat and watched it happen," I said. "Are you saying that Val and I somehow changed your minds?"

"There were some in our ruling council who felt your species was advancing too fast technologically for your own good. These advocated that we… reset your civilization until you had grown enough as a species to take care of some of your own problems."

"Reset. That doesn't sound like a good thing." I tried to keep Krizon talking, while keeping my remarks to a minimum. His logical remarks had veered away from the bombshells he'd dropped on me, and I wasn't sure if it was evasion, or that he just didn't get what he'd done to me.

I felt betrayed all over again by this being who thought I would be a great lab experiment and then abandoned me to be raised by robots… *Who I loved.* Damnit! This was all I needed, one more way to feel that I couldn't trust anyone or anything.

"It was not. I was adamantly against resetting your world," Krizon continued, oblivious to my emotions. "It would have slowed your planet's technological progress by centuries, possibly causing you to become vulnerable to the same self-destruction that we had been fighting to avoid."

I humored Krizon—I kept nodding—when I wanted to hit him.

It won't help my case.

"When it was found," he continued, "that our two species, with minor genetic manipulation, were compatible, the idea of resetting your advance was replaced with almost the exact opposite strategy."

"What is it with you Dallies, and your desire to be the 'fathers' of the galaxy?"

Krizon turned back to me with his pupil-less eyes, and I could swear I saw another emotion on his usually mask-like face. Sadness.

"This is something that is not generally known, Tanner, but our people, being incredibly long-lived by Terran standards, are paying a price for being such an elder species. We are stagnating."

This didn't sound good. "Stagnating?"

"The last pure-blooded Laldoralin was born 375 of your solar years ago. We had hoped, like some of the elder races that are no longer existent, that we would ascend to some higher form of being. While this has happened for a few of our people, most of us wind up following the well-known path to that end. We simply die, like everything else in this universe. Our species will be extinct with the next ten of your solar centuries."

Sobering news indeed. Personal issues aside, anyone who wasn't a total isolationist nut job, could see that the Dallies had not only done a lot for Earth, but for most of the species in the space that they called the Hegemony.

They had kept us from destroying ourselves, and my interstellar studies classes had taught that they'd done this on more than one occasion across the Hegemony. They'd preserved species, advanced them into a union across this part of the galaxy, and built that union into a thriving trading alliance.

They were a parent species that often kept the toddlers from burning down their own houses. They took that as their responsibility and they took it very seriously.

"So, you are trying to live on through the younger races?"

"In a way. Aside from fertility issues, our genome has much to offer, and who knows? Perhaps we can help other species avoid the fate that now faces us. We are a very long-lived people. You, Tanner, will probably far outlive every natural human you know, barring violent demise. You also are much more resistant to diseases, as are all of our hybrid children. We do intend it as a way that some of what we are can continue, but we also intend it as a gift."

"Well, I'm not sure I see the gift in being left in stasis for a century and a half, though. Val and I were more science experiments than offspring."

"You do not see, because you are so very, very young by Laldoralin standards. Because you have not yet lived long enough to see the long game. If you think of it, which do you believe the better time for you to be alive would be, now or the "Crazy Years" of your 21st century? Which do you think you would have thrived better in?"

"That's a loaded question. You could have taken us with you."

"At the time, the Laldoralin were engaged in stopping the Klugg from preying on some of your core-ward neighbors. I could not have taken you and your sister with me, as our success was not a certain thing. Stasis was my solution, my son. I did not see the pain it might cause you later.

"As I said, Krizon, you are a master of understatement. Human offspring need emotional attachment. It keeps us from growing up to cause the kind of problems you say you want to prevent in our species."

"Our emotions have cooled over the years and we have forgotten how such things might affect. Tanner, I am sorry for the pain this has caused you."

Dammit. I had a long diatribe ready to throw in his face, and then he gives me what appears to be a sincere apology. But I had realized something. Whatever emotional support I wanted from this being just wasn't ever going to happen. He was incapable. I wanted yell at him, but what would be the point? The only real parent Val and I ever had was Ron, and I was grateful for him. My fury dissipated into sadness.

This was a waste of time.

"I'm sorry, too. However, I'm sure you didn't come all this way to salve my wounded feelings. I've been moved to active duty on the *Seeker*, and I'm told that you are the reason. I'm surprised after all you've told me about my 'value,' that you'd want me on a risky exploratory mission."

"Are you familiar with the term 'hot house flower', Tanner?"

"Yes." I replied. "Are you saying I've become pampered, somehow? Because I'm not seeing it."

"The *Seeker*, and her sister ships the *Searcher* and the *Wanderer* are all seeking new frontiers. All other human endeavors are simply seeking to catch up to the rest of the races in known space. Your career paths, if you were not on any of these vessels, would be treading ground that has already been trod. Being a scientist in a lab is not for you, being a defense force soldier who seldom ventures far from your own system is not for you. Only by being placed in the unknown can our hybrid children reach their potential."

"And my sister? Did you get her the posting on the *Wanderer*?"

"You need not worry about Valiel. Yes, she has been posted to the *Wanderer*. Having graduated a year earlier than you, I was able to make sure she made it on to that ship as an academy graduate, telling her the same things that I have told you not long ago. As for you, I had to, as you say on Earth, 'pull strings' to get you on the *Seeker*."

This had to be the most parental thing Krizon had ever done, as far as I knew. He was trying to meddle in my life.

In this case, I saw that fighting it would not get me anything that I wanted. The truth was, I was excited to be posted to the *Seeker*, and I knew my anger had little to do with what Krizon had done to get me there, my problem was with him. I also realized that burying him under recriminations wouldn't be useful to either of us.

"I see. I will try not to disappoint. But understand, I'm not going to be doing anything for the express reason of making you proud. Whatever I do, I will be doing for my own reasons, to excel because I feel that's what I want to do."

"Nonetheless, my son, I will be proud of you. May your life be long and content."

I saluted and left the room.

Chapter Seven

When I left the 'interview' I had to admit my emotions were just as mixed up as when I'd come aboard, just in different ways. Everything Krizon said was very logical, but that was the problem, wasn't it? It had been all carefully thought out, but there was no... feeling... in the decisions.

I was halfway back to the runabout when I was 'ambushed' in the hallway.

"Look at him, Evan. He's an adult now, and so handsome!" a voice said, bringing me to an abrupt halt.

"By the galaxy, Dora, he looks good! Our boy looks ready for adventure."

It occurred to me that I hadn't had this much parental attention all at once in over a century and a half.

"Dora? Evan?" I queried the air around me.

Two human-form holograms leapt into light-based existence around me.

"Tanner! We didn't want you to leave without saying goodbye." Dora said.

Ever have one of those moments where you are so conflicted that you literally do not know what to think? How to react? This was one of those.

"I... uh... so. You're both AIs I understand."

Awkward.

"Of course, dear," Dora said. "From what we heard of your conversation with Krizon, you didn't know?"

"You were listening?"

Both of them looked toward the other's projection, which was probably for my benefit, as were their sheepish looks.

"We aren't really supposed to eavesdrop, especially on Krizon or the prime shipboard commander, but this was a special case, son," Evan said. "It's been so long since we interfaced, we were very much wanting to see you."

"I really wish you wouldn't call me that."

I knew I had upset them, because instead of manufactured expressions, both holograms simply froze, like computers that've tried to analyze something poorly coded. They stood that way for a few moments, then Dora snapped back to animation first, an expression on her face that was a very convincing facsimile of righteous anger.

"Tanner Voss! How dare you!" she said. "Evan and I are the best parents you EVER had. That we are 'artificial' and were in android bodies does not change that, nor the fact that we both love you more than our own existence!"

"Yeah. I'd guess the Laldoralin programmed you that way."

"Evan and I are full citizens of the Hegemony, young man. We are independent beings, no matter what our assignment was. Whether our programing came from AI specialists or flesh and blood mothers and fathers, we still consider you our son, and nothing, no matter how cruel you are to us, will change that!"

Dammit. I wanted to launch into a flying snit, but the truth was, no matter what their origins were, Evan and Dora had always been there for Val and me, no matter what the problem. AIs or not, I believed her when she said they loved me. Or, at least their programs got as close as a digital being could.

And I felt like a creep.

When I thought about it, with my looking down on them for being programs… who programmed Val and me? Dora and Evan. It was a strange way to look at relationships I admit, but I decided I didn't care about their origins. They were there for us.

Krizon wasn't.

"I… um… I'm sorry, Mom. You were the only mother I ever had, and truth be told, you were really good at it," I said. I turned toward Evan but his hologram had disappeared.

"Evan, please," Dora said. "He's young, he's been through some shocks recently. Please, dear."

Nothing. Dora's image looked at me imploringly.

"Dad?" I said to the ceiling of the hallway. "I'm sorry. I'm very sorry."

He appeared, though he didn't step forward. "I understand, son.

But we've missed you so much in the time that's passed. It was just a little bit more than I could handle, you not thinking that we love you."

"I do love you both," I said, before I even thought about the implications of my words. "I… there's just been so much to take in today. Krizon, new revelations about you two, and of course, huge life change with the new job."

It struck me that grown children had probably been saying similar things to cover for poor behavior for millennia.

I sure had an odd family.

Chapter Eight

"*Seeker*, this is shuttle Monte Cristo, requesting permission to enter hanger," Nguyen said. We had left the *LV Kaialai*, and were en route to our final destination.

"Monte Cristo, this is Seeker shuttle hanger. Doors are opening, and we've cleared some space for you. Try not to break anything, Vinh."

"I don't get no respect," my pilot replied. We entered the bay, and through an atmospheric containment field, I saw two heavy-duty cargo shuttles against the back bulkhead. The Monte Cristo passed through the field and landed in the available space in front of them, which wasn't much. Nguyen placed the shuttle down without so much as a scratch. He turned to me and shook my hand. "Thanks, pardner, I've never seen the inside of a Dallie ship before. Pretty interesting."

"Thanks for the ride. It was mondo smooth," I said, grabbing my kit and heading for the opening hatch. "Safe travels!"

"Safe travels to you too, cadet. Hope it goes well for you."

As the door closed behind me and the shuttle began to lift for departure, a petite, shaven-headed officer marched my way at full tilt. Stopping in front of me as I snapped to attention, she looked up at me with an expression that one might use for a booger on one's shoe. Evidently my stop-over on a Laldoralin vessel didn't impress her in the least.

"Finally here, are we, cadet?" she said. "Grab your gear and follow me. The XO wants to see you."

"Sorry to be late, Lieutenant, I was delayed by the Laldoralin vessel. Cadet Tanner Voss reporting for duty."

"I am well aware of your detour, Cadet. I'm referring to the fact that this ship was supposed to leave for the rendezvous with our sister ships well outside the plane of the ecliptic, yesterday at 13:00 hours. But command said we had to wait. For you. As you might guess, everyone was thrilled by the news."

Oh, Creator of all the Universe, can it get any worse?

I should know by now never to ask that question.

She quick-marched me through several corridors in a set of branching turns I could never hope to recreate, into a lift, up several decks and stopped at a door with a plaque that read 'Commander M'Buku.' She hit the door chime and an intercom voice said, "Enter."

The door opened, and across a fairly plain-looking but very functional desk, the Executive Officer looked up from his CommPadd. Commander M'Buku was a big man, with a weathered face that bespoke a lot of experience. He looked at us with interest.

"Lieutenant LeCosta reporting, SIR! I have our last-minute addition with me as you commanded."

"I know who you are, LeCosta," the commander said with an amused tone. "You really don't need to announce yourself every time we interface." He looked at the CommPadd on my belt. "Is that a student Padd? Lieutenant, please make sure that our young friend here has a standard ship's Padd issued, would you? I will copy his duty roster and billet to you also."

"To me, sir? Er… why to me?" she asked.

"Because, LeCosta, you are the soul of efficiency, and this is a matter of more delicacy that you might think. Only one of my best people can do this in a manner that will serve the ship to its best end. That's why I want you to take Tanner here under your wing and make sure that he becomes a useful member of this crew. I'm depending on you."

I made every effort to hide my grimace at LeCosta's commendation. She certainly hadn't impressed me with her confidentiality or professionalism. I watched her petite form inflate with the praise, then deflate slightly when she realized she'd been saddled with keeping an eye on me for the trip. I filed the commander's technique under Advanced Manipulation skills.

"Yes sir. Thank you, sir."

"Now, I need to speak with the cadet privately for a few moments, if you don't mind waiting in the corridor."

As she turned from him, the look she gave me stated she damn well did mind, but *she* knew how to follow orders. The look also seemed to obliquely question the need for me to exist. I was an irritation to her, and somehow, I found that satisfying.

"Welcome aboard, Mr. Voss. I am Commander M'Buku. I hope the lieutenant there didn't barbecue you too badly when you joined us."

"Only lightly seared, sir. I am excited by the opportunity to serve aboard the *Seeker*."

"Good. Excitement is good. However, I want you to know that you are going to be one busy young man. We are expecting you to complete your academy training, but no one on this ship has light duty shifts. You will be expected to study your lessons after your shifts are over, though some of your hands-on training will obviously be happening while you work." He looked down at his Padd. "Also, as you are undoubtedly aware, you were placed on this vessel, not only because your father is a Laldoralin VIP, but also because of, from what I can see here, is an incredible talent for gunnery."

"Yes, sir."

"Maybe we'll get to see some of that... skill in some test firings. Hopefully we won't need it in reality, but we are going far out there. I'm happy for any advantage we can get. To be honest, I'm rather fascinated by this talent you possess."

"I won't disappoint you, sir."

"I've asked our Chief Engineer, Commander Solas, to assign you a place in engineering, so you'll need to interface with him. He can be a bit touchy about his jump drive and FTL engines, so try not to take it personally. You will also spend a minimum of six hours per week on the emergency bridge, learning our weapon systems under the tutelage of Chief Kurakin. She can be a harsh taskmaster also, but she really knows those systems and how to use them. You will report to her Monday, Wednesday, and Friday at the Secondary Bridge, 11:00 hours. When she's through with you, you'll be able to make the weapons on this ship sit up and purr."

"Yes, sir," I said, marveling at the smoothness of his mixed metaphors. "Sir, is there some sort of map or chart of the ship? I quite literally was given no time for in-depth learning about this vessel. I was re-assigned less than twenty-four hours ago."

"You'll find everything you need on your new Padd. It interfaces with the ship's library system, and will answer almost any question you have."

"Thank you, sir."

"That's all I had, Cadet. You are dismissed."

"Aye sir," I said, making my way to the door. Once in the corridor, I found LeCosta leaning against a wall, giving me the stank eye. She was not taking being my handler very well.

"Hello, EllTee. I'm done in there." I said, cheerfully.

"I can see that, Voss. Give me a moment," She said. She tapped her own CommPadd and said. "P-3, wherefore art thou, Bot?" She read something on her screen, and clipped the Padd back to her belt. "Cool your thrusters a moment, Cadet. He's almost here."

He turned out to be a small float-bot. In one of his claws, which hung down like those of an owl, he carried a new-looking CommPadd, which I assumed was for me. I was proven correct when P-3 extended an arm and handed it to me.

"You can finish set-up in your quarters, Voss. Once you do, I want you to study everything about this ship and take a stroll around to learn the lay-out. I do *not* intend to nursemaid you, and I expect to not have to answer questions that you can learn from your device. Am I clear?"

"Crystal, ma'am."

"Good answer. Now, I'm going to take you to your quarters and introduce you to your roommates. Then, I'm going to expect you to function on your own until I contact you again."

"Understood."

"Oh, and Voss? The XO assigned me to keep an eye on you, and I will be doing that, but… one last thing…"

"Yes?"

"Don't make me look bad."

❖

We dropped down three decks, and passed a sign that read "Entering Ship's Safe Core."

"Safe Core?" I said. "What does that mean?"

"I guess that I shouldn't be surprised that someone who's only ever crewed on a twenty-year-old trainer like the *Condor* wouldn't know modern ship survival design," LeCosta snarked. "The Safe Core is like a ship within a ship. Medical, Replication, Stores, Engineering, and the E-Bridge are all down here in the heavily armored bullet core of the *Seeker*. It's where we evac to in case of catastrophic emergency. Most crew quarters are here, too. If you'd been paying attention when you entered the shuttle hanger, you'd have seen the extra thick hull that surrounds that too."

I felt my face color a little, but reminded myself I'd had several shocks in the last few days and might've not been at my attention-paying best. At this point, I decided to do what LeCosta probably wanted me to do anyway. I stopped asking questions and decided to find our everything I could from the Library System.

Ten doors down on the outer corridor of the Core, we stopped at door number 221. I wanted to comment that it was too bad it wasn't on B-deck, but I doubt she would have gotten the Sherlock Holmes reference. From what I had seen of her so far, she might not have gotten it even if I explained, and I was not in the mood for more scathing commentary.

We opened the door, and a large man with short-cropped black hair came off his bunk and went to attention.

"At ease, Crewman Fonseca. This is your new roommate, Cadet Tanner Voss. He'll be finishing his last year of academy onboard and I would appreciate it if you would help me keep him out of trouble."

"Glad to, Lieutenant, but shouldn't he be in officer country? Not down here slumming with us crew people?"

"As I said, he's a cadet, not yet an officer." LeCosta looked over at me with half-lowered eyelids "Lower in rank than anyone serving here except the civilian scientists and their aids. Where is Crewman Chikit?"

"Stepped out to the commissary for a snack. Zhitins tend to need snacks pretty often."

"You can introduce Voss here to him. I'm leaving him in your tender care." LeCosta turned and went out the door.

"She's not the friendliest, is she?" Fonseca seemed to read my mind.

"Is she always this warm and welcoming?"

"Brand new lieutenant, junior grade," he replied. "Worried that they'll find a reason to demote her back to ensign, and that tends to make her overcompensate and drive everyone under her half-crazy." Fonseca shrugged his big shoulders. "It's actually what she does best."

"You got that last part right."

"So, you're a cadet, hunh? How's that work?"

I didn't know how much I was allowed to say, so I went tactical-vague. "I dunno. For some reason they seem to think I've got something special goin' on. Guess you'd have to ask the higher-ups."

Not specifically lying, or at least only a lie of omission.

"No thanks. Officers have been getting more and more like officers as we get ready to get this show on the road and head out for the rendezvous. I think they're starting to stress." He eyed me for a moment. "Just between you an' me, of course."

"From my experience so far, we're in complete agreement," I told him. "So, our roommate is a Zhitin? Are there many E.T. crew on board? I thought this was *Earth's* big push to the stars."

"You did jumps in your academy trainer, didn't you?" Fonseca asked.

"Of course! I was just starting fourth year, and…"

"And what happened when you came out of Nth space?" He smiled and raised his bushy eyebrows, waiting for my response.

"Well, for most of the crew, what usually happens. The automated systems take over because the crew is temporarily too dizzy to function, an effect of the Nth space passage."

"Yeah," he continued. "And you know what? That is the fault of our jump drive design. The Dallies know what the problem is, but they say we have to figure it out ourselves. No medals for mediocrity. But most of the E.T. crew-persons on this ship, their species don't have this problem. It seems that humans just have a predisposition for that scrambling of our senses after a jump and they're here to take over from their human counterparts while the human crew is getting their space legs back."

"Well, I don't have as much of a problem with that, being part E.T...."

"Really?"

I pulled back the slightly long hair on the side of my hair and exposed the points of my ears.

"Wow, who...?"

"My father is Laldoralin."

"Aw, man, I hope I didn't offend you with that 'Dallie' comment. I just..."

"I call 'em that too, Emil. Hadn't seen my real father for a century and a half." I realize I had just given too much info, when Fonseca began to look at my face very intently. His easy-going manner had made me relax my guard.

"Oh, man, you're the kid... the one they found in the stasis chamber, aren't you?"

"Ah... yeah. My sister and I."

He sat there, looked at me for a moment, touched my shoulder and said, "Hey, Tanner. As a representative of the human race, I'd like to totally apologize for those stupid 'Home Bodies' and all their species-ist bullshit."

I felt my face begin to grow warm, and mumbled, "Well, they went after us so much, my foster dad moved us to the wilds of New Zealand. I had a scare today with a bunch of protestors. I was just trying to get to the New Phoenix shuttle, and had to make a run for my train."

"Buncha crazy frightened gizzbutts, who see change as terrifying. What they fear, they attack," Fonseca said, a bitter expression on his face. "You'd think, after this much information from and about other species flowing in from across the Hegemony, they'd realize diversity is something to embrace, not go all 'frightened monkeys flinging poo,' but I guess that's too much to ask of a certain section of humankind. Though honestly, I'm beginning to think there's just a big grouping of Neanderthals hiding in amongst the homo sapiens."

"That's kinda being insulting to Neanderthals," I said. The truth was, the members of the Earth For Earth movement had been tactically methodical on more than one of their attempts to murder Valiel and myself.

They'd come close the second time, and that was when EarthGov had made sure that we both had bodyguards. There were other species and hybrids on Earth, but for some reason the E.F.E. had made us their demon poster children. We were by no means the first aliens the inhabitants of Earth had seen, or the first hybrids. It was the knowledge that the Laldoralin had been mixing gene pools as early as the mid-21st century that had set them off. We became a symbol of a mixed galaxy, something they hated.

And they were good at hating.

They'd also opposed everything Earth was doing to take our place among the Galactic Alliance of Systems, sometimes quite violently.

My experience in Portland hadn't done anything to make me think they might relent. I'd have gladly seen them all instantly translocated to a distant point in the galaxy. Maybe even another galaxy.

"This behavior is common in emerging races," buzzing metallic voices said. "It will pass eventually, as you humans evolve beyond it."

"Tanner, this is Chikit, our other roommate."

"I greet you," Chikit said. He was one of the Zhitin species, an insectavroid race that had been part of the Hegemony for many years. They, galactic distance-wise, were fairly close neighbors with Earth, originating on the fourth planet of the star we call Gliese 581. Chikit had one of his pairs of arms folded to his sides, while the two other pairs gesticulated in front of him. His was a species that communicated through gesture, and it was fortunate that his CommPadd provided a real-time translation. He lowered himself onto his bunk which looked like a cross between a hammock and a bathtub.

"I greet you in return, Chikit. You are the first of your species that I have encountered," I said, using the standard greeting when meeting a member of a species unfamiliar to oneself. "I regret any mistakes I make in advance."

"I forgive your mistakes and hope you will forgive my own," he said, reciting the standard response. "You said that you are part Laldoralin? An honor of meeting you is mine then. My species was determinedly upon a path of self-immolation when the Laldoralin, in essence, helped us to see a wiser path. We also went through a xenophobic bio-weapon age, and had it not been for them, we would have destroyed all life on our world. From what I understand, something similar happened with Earth."

"I am glad to know that your world was saved." I was so damned happy not to be the weird one anymore. Wait, that sounds species-ist, but I didn't mean it that way. I just meant I was so glad not to stand out and to be in a diverse group. It felt like I finally belonged somewhere. Everyone was welcome and it had nothing to do with DNA and everything to do with ability. I had to prove myself like everyone else. I relished the opportunity.

"Well, no need to treat me as special. I just…" I was interrupted by an incoming comm chime from my Padd.

"Voss? This is LeCosta. Have you started your exploration of the ship, yet?"

"Er… No, ma'am." It felt weird to call her that; she couldn't have been more than a few years older than I was. "I was just meeting my second roommate, Chikit, and…"

"You can get acquainted later. I've assigned P-3 to nursemaid you around for a while, for the safety of the ship and all aboard her."

Oh, you're very funny, boss.

"Yes ma'am."

"He tells me he's waiting outside your cabin. Get to it. LeCosta out."

I looked at my roomies. "Gotta go."

"Good luck, Cadet. Don't worry though, you'll do fine," Fonseca said.

"Hopefully."

Chapter Nine

P-3 was indeed waiting outside.

"Greetings, Cadet. I have been instructed to assist in any way you may need to familiarize yourself with the vessel and her mission." Instead of an authoritative male voice, a warm female voice came from the small floatbot.

"I thought you had a male protocol, P-3. Lt. LeCosta always refers to you as 'he,' does she not?"

"I am gender neutral, Cadet. You may have noticed that I am a machine, and not a bio-sentient. Lt. LeCosta responds better to a baritone voice, while your psychological profile suggest you will be better able to interface with a female alto vocalization. Would you like to specify another voice mode? There are several options to choose from."

"Actually, I'm used to the male voice now, let's stick with that. Can you suggest a 'tour' of the Seeker that will inform, and eventually end at the Library?"

"Affirmative. If you will follow me, I will act as guide." P-3 floated down the corridor and turned starboard in a cross hallway. Our first stop was engine room Alpha. This housed the Faster Than Light drive which we'd use to cover distance after making our jumps through Nth space. In established jump routes, emergence could be a pretty precise science. But in new routes, you could emerge from a jump light years away from your target. Even highly developed math models couldn't seem to correct for 'drift' because Nth space simply wouldn't cooperate.

The FTL drive would allow us to reach destinations from our jump 'landing site' to the actual target in a reasonable amount of time. Once we reached our destination for that jump, actual spatial coordinates could then be calculated at both ends, allowing for much more precise jump travel.

"Excuse me," a voice called out from behind me. "What are you doing in my engine room?" I turned to see a very thin, very fit, very bald man wearing commander rank, bearing down on me. "Oh. I see. The cadet."

My popularity level was holding steady.

"Are you Commander Solas, sir?" I said, snapping to attention.

"Yes, Cadet, I am. And according to my duty roster, you are not scheduled to report until 1800 hours tomorrow, after you meet with Chief Kurakin."

"Lt. LeCosta tasked me with guiding the cadet on a familiarity tour, sir," P-3 interceded. "It was my calculation that the best place to start such an outing would be the most important parts of the ship, thus we began in main engineering."

Evidently, they were programming our mechanical assistants with tact and diplomacy modules now.

"All right. Since he's to be part of my team, get on with it. But don't bother or interrupt anyone in their work. You can ask questions tomorrow, when I've decided where I want someone of cadet-level skills working. I assure you, it won't be around these precious engines. Dismissed."

"Aye, Commander." I gave my smartest salute. He walked off shaking his head, and P-3 continued the tour, showing me the various configurable workstations and explaining to me where each side corridor and crawlway went. I resolved to have all these memorized by the time I left the library today.

"You are picking up things quite well, are you not, Cadet Voss?" A pleasant female voice said from behind me.

I turned to see a young woman who appeared to be a Laldoralin. Very tall, with elf-like features and slightly metallic-looking bronze skin. Her short-cropped hair had a purple tint, but that could've been cosmetic.

"I believe so, Chief. Begging your pardon, ma'am. I didn't think there were any Laldoralin aboard."

"I am Shendra Zahn. I am like you, a halfling. My mother was Kiffer."

My memory of my xeno-bio studies told me that the Kiffer, a humanoid species from the far side of the Hegemony, came from a planet near a binary star, but I couldn't dredge up the name of the star itself. Most likely because it was so far away from Earth it didn't have a human designation. Embarrassing.

"I'm pleased to meet another that I have that in common with. You are the first of your species that I have encountered, and I regret…"

"Do not worry, please, young Vossling. The Kiffer are known for our sense of humor. I am delighted to meet you and hope that we will be able to become better acquainted soon. My sister Zuala is Second Medical Officer aboard. She will want to meet you as well. She has a strong interest in mixing Laldoralin hybrid gene pools. You will like her."

What?

"I… er… That's interesting."

"I am sure that she will want for me to be involved also, but as I am above you in your direct chain of command, that might not be appropriate. At this time, anyway."

"I… I…"

"Excuse me Tanner Voss. I must resume my duties now."

"Yes ma'am." I watched as she turned and walked off toward a duty station.

"You have made an impression I believe, Cadet." P-3 noted.

"What… what just happened?"

"Are you unaware of how gene pools are intermixed, Mr. Voss? Our library system has extensive…"

"I have more than a theoretical knowledge of how that is done, P-3. Thank you very much."

"You are welcome, Cadet Voss. I am glad to be of service."

We left engineering and visited the jump drive room, and I couldn't help but notice there were armed guards near the drive stations. Sticking my head back in the FTL section, I noticed there were also security personnel on the catwalks above the FTL drive.

"P-3, why all of the armed security people?"

"There is a threat of E.F.E. interference."

"What? I'm assuming everyone on these ships have been vetted six ways to Sunday," I said, incredulous.

"Personnel and staff in the Galactic Consulate are also heavily screened," P-3 said. "However, two years ago a bomb almost destroyed several of the ambassadors on that premises. The Earth For Earth contingent has grown sophisticated over the decades, and their operatives are well-hidden, and well trained."

"Okay, as it's unlikely that that Commander Solas is going to assign me to the jump drive section, let's move along." I said. I was trying not to let it show, but I was seething inside. I really hated the E.F.E. Not only had they made my life hell, but now they were trying to force their version of reality on humanity and its next big step. Were it not for these jack holes, I imagined that the atmosphere on the *Seeker* would be a lot less tense.

After a tour of the commissary, sick bay, Remora hanger, and science sections, we finally came to the secondary command bridge, deep in the Safe Core.

"Access denied," the ship's computer told me in its mellifluous voice.

"Hopefully this will be cleared up before I show up for my duty shift tomorrow morning," I said.

As we roamed the corridors, we passed officers and crew and quite a few of them gave me interested looks or raised eyebrows. I was praying to whatever made the universe that it was my cadet uniform, and not in recognition of my status as minor celebrity, the kid from the 21st century. No one wants to be the pink monkey.

We finally ended the tour at the library section, and I took a seat in front of a multi-display, and logged in by holding my Comm-Padd to the keypad and laying my hand on a scan-panel. I was enveloped in a blue scan light for a moment, and the computer said. "Access granted, Cadet Tanner Voss."

I began trying to familiarize myself with the *Seeker's* design and operations. Finally, after about an hour of general studies, I tried to access the operations of the tactical station, thinking there might be some simulations I could run to have a leg up when I met Chief Kurakin for tomorrow's shift.

Access denied.

"P-3, I'm supposed to start tactical gunnery lessons tomorrow, and I can't access anything on the tactical stations. Is there any way that you can ping LeCosta and ask her if I can be authorized?"

I swear, my floatBot colleague hesitated.

"Is there a problem, P-3?"

"Please forgive me, Cadet Voss, but there has been a lapse in my programming. I should have warned you about accessing systems you are not authorized to use. I expect in a moment or two, a member of security is going to show up to find out who has violated that protocol."

"Oh crap! Now what do I do?"

"You explain yourself, mister." A low-pitched female voice said from the doorway.

She was a Valkyrie. There was no other description half as apt. At least 6'3, short cut blonde hair, broad strong shoulders, and yes, I'm just going to say it. She was gorgeous.

She also looked about to kick my butt, and I had a strong suspicion she could do it with little trouble.

I was out of my chair, and at attention at roughly the speed of light. "Ma'am! This cadet is scheduled for training on the tactical grid tomorrow with Chief Kurakin. I didn't realize I was unauthorized for access to that information."

"The error is mine, Chief," P-3 interceded. "I did not apprise the cadet beforehand about what he shouldn't access. I will report this lapse to my programmers."

She didn't answer, instead walking past us both and examining the screens I had floating above my station. She turned, and there was just the ghost of a smile on her face. I took this as a possibility I might not wind up in the brig.

"Computer," she said, "grant Cadet Voss access to all tactical station information and access to the secondary command center and its tactical station. Authorization Kurakin-782."

"Acknowledged," the computer replied. "Cadet Voss has been granted access to the proscribed systems."

She turned to me. "As you may have gathered, Cadet, I will be your instructor. I'm Kurakin. I'll see you tomorrow, 11:00 hours sharp. See what you can learn of the systems before then. They're a bit more advanced than what you've been exposed to, but from what I've been told, you're a quick study."

"Shall I practice in the secondary bridge?"

"No, just sim here. I'd prefer, even in simulation, that you be under supervision when on Bridge 2."

"Aye, Chief. I'll sim here."

She nodded, and walked out.

"She's the tactical officer. And she's in security?" I asked P-3.

"Though a non-commissioned officer, she is the secondary lead in the tactical division. She is also first in command in the security section. Chief Kurakin is quite capable."

"Not to mention beautiful."

"I will have to take your word on that, Cadet Voss. She's not really my type."

I looked closely at P-3 for a moment. Most of our Earth-designed AIs did not have a sense of humor. Evidently, this generation of XM34 FloatBots was an exception. I turned back to my screens, and asked the computer to configure the layout as an approximation of the tactical station. A quick once over showed me that while they weren't quite the same layout I was familiar with, and there were definitely a few unrecognizables, I could figure out their usage.

I had the computer give me attack scenarios that were based on actual events from the Laldoralin database, and ran through situation after situation. The *Seeker's* defense systems were robust to say the least. Small point defense energy pulse pods covered every zone around the ship, and though they were considered 'short range' beam weapons they packed a punch and there were a lot of them. In several of the scenarios, I used them for targets farther than spec recommended and, according to the computer, they did the job just fine.

The primary weapons were particle beams, using an ionized stream laced with gamma particles and a few other things I was not privy to. Unlike the time when I was born, the schematics for every deadly device weren't available on the world info-web. I put the simulated weapons through a number of experiments, firing at farther and farther away simulated targets. They were deadly at even distances of half a million miles.

The gunnery stations were actually a three-person set-up, and I was sure that if I was on the bridge, I would be at the third station, with oversight from the officers above me, but in simulation, I was able to make all the decisions for myself.

"Wow. These main guns pack a serious wallop. You could open an unshielded ship like a foil-covered baked potato," I said aloud.

"All weapon systems are retractable into the main hull," P-3 informed me.

"I'd guess that cuts down on maintenance."

"Possibly, though that is not the reason. If this expedition meets another race, one unknown to Earth or the Hegemony, it would be in everyone's best interest not to appear threatening, unless threatened by the new contact. Extended weapons are a sign of aggressive intent."

"Guess it's a good idea to hide one's strength unless it's needed."

"Indeed. Cadet Voss. You should familiarize yourself with the missile system, also. And the rail gun, though that is primarily intended for mining."

"The missiles have an automated firing system P-3, so I assume it's 'point in the general direction of the target' and let fly. Unless you can control them manually?"

"It is not common procedure to manually control their flight path, but it is possible."

I sat up in my chair. This was something I'd never seen at the academy. Of course, it was probably a good idea to have safeguards and digital assists when students are at the firing controls. But this wasn't the academy.

"Show me how to go manual with those missiles, P-3!"

Chapter Ten

After another couple hours, I realized I was starving. Assuring P-3 I was good, I cut my keeper loose and headed toward the commissary. Checking my Padd, I walked two hallways core-ward, got turned around for a moment, then headed back toward the bow of the ship. Another port-side turn and I was at the food center.

There were several people in the mess, almost all Terran. I didn't see anyone I knew, which wasn't surprising, but I was very conscious of my cadet uniform. Most of the crew were in standard military everyday dress, with some the engineering staff in coveralls. Every uniform had a small patch with a the 'logo' for the Seeker. Everyone except me, that is. Hopefully I could at least get that rectified.

I was sitting by myself when a mechanical voice said. "Voss. You are assigned to me."

I looked around but I couldn't see anyone near me, and no one seemed to be looking my way. Imagine my surprise when a pair of mechanical "fingers" appeared on the opposite side of my table and a small hairy figure pulled itself into a chair. It was about the size of a raccoon, but looked much more like a small terrestrial sloth, if sloths were hued in colors of orange and red. Wearing what looked like a mesh body suit under a child-sized exoskeleton with a number of extendable devices, the small being pulled itself partway on the table and looked at me with large limpid eyes. I saw a lieutenant's pip on the suit.

"Um… Sir?" I said.

Through a vocoder, it said. "I am Truval, lieutenant rank. You. Assigned to my section. Duty shift starts at 18:00 hours in robotics. You will be there?"

"Sir. Yes, sir! I will report to robotics at 18:00 hours tomorrow." Evidently Commander Solas had decided where to pawn me off. I had only a slight idea where robotics was, but I had a Padd and a digital map. I'd be there.

"All hands," a female voice over the loudspeaker system interrupted us before Truval could continue. "This is the captain. Prepare to leave orbit for the rendezvous point. Once there, we will join our sister ships for jump drive testing. Secure all stations."

"Ah," Truval said. "Yamashita Captain has been eager to… how do Terrans say? Get this show on the road."

"Sir, am I to understand that the jump drive hasn't really been tested in actuality?"

"There have been many simulations. Drive itself not tested in reality we are existing in," Truval told me. "I scent nervousness from you, young being. Jump drives have been around a long period. No need for fear."

"Yes, sir," I replied. To say I was completely reassured about an untested jump drive would be less than truthful. I felt mild gravitational shifts, then the ship was filled with a background hum, meaning we were done with thrusters, and the main FTL drive was taking us out of our orbit.

"But Earth-built drives are somewhat of a new thing," I said, "and from what I hear, not all of the bugs are ironed out."

"There are no insects in the drive. Your fears are unfounded." I had forgotten a cardinal rule when dealing with non-Terran races: don't use slang.

"Aye, sir. May I ask what part of robotics I will be assigned to?"

"Lieutenant Danforth and Chief Moreland handle in-ship bots, and are protective of them. You will join Chief Pickens and staff in maintaining the Remora flight."

"Aye, sir. I look forward to the assignment."

"You are polishing the fruit, Cadet?"

"What? Oh. No, sir. I was worried I'd wind up scrubbing down the repair bay. I am quite happy to be working on a part of the ship with some challenge to it."

"Lucky for you, bots take on cleaning duties. I have read your record and transcripts, at least parts not blacked out. You are competent and trained, but room for improvement. I will see you improve, I owe this to up and coming ones. You will make best effort to learn fast."

"I won't disappoint you, sir."

"18:00 hours, tomorrow," he said and dropped back to the floor. Four extendable legs sprouted from the exoskeleton and he walked away.

So far today my number of encounters with off-worlders is about even with my interaction with Terrans.

I wandered over to the food dispensation area and looked through the hologram menu. I had assumed we'd be eating institutional food, but the food printing system on the Seeker was top-notch. I sat down with a freshly replicated avocado steak and sweet potato fries when Fonseca wandered in. He waved, went to the food distiller, then joined me.

"I guess we're finally under way," I said. "Sorry I delayed everyone."

"Ahhh. We've been waiting for four weeks, man. Don't sweat an extra eight hours. You find your duty stations?"

"Yes, I train tactical with Chief Kurakin in the morning, and work on the Remoras with Lieutenant Truval in the afternoon."

"Ah. The warrior goddess and the teddy bear. You do live an interesting life. Kurakin is a harsh task-mistress. Truval, while expecting your best, tends to be a little more... mentorly."

"He does kind of remind me of a fuzzy Master Yoda." I said. Emil looked at me blankly, and I was reminded yet again of the erosion of time on humanity's memory. "He was a cultural icon back in my time. Er... my birth time. He was a Jedi master."

"You mean like that cult in Denmark? Running around with fire-blades and playing with magnetic displacement gloves?"

"Really?" I asked. "I hadn't heard of them."

Emil was about to expand upon this bit of modern history I'd missed when another crewman walked in. He started toward the food distillers when he saw me and stopped short.

"Uh-oh," Fonseca whispered, "Chief Moreland."

As he approached, my friend stood and saluted, even though Moreland wasn't an officer. Seeing which way the wind blew, I followed suit. The man was wearing Master Chief rank, and judging from Emil's quick reaction, he expected instant respect protocol.

"At ease, Fonseca," he said, not acknowledging my salute. "You must be Voss."

"Yes, Master Chief," I said.

"What the hell is this corps coming to, when a flipping cadet winds up crewing on a class A-1 mission?" he said. "This is ridiculous. Everyone here worked hard to be selected for this."

"Yes Chief. I understand that…"

"But you, little cadet, wind up on our mission because you have connections with the Lalliedallies. Scuttlebutt is your daddy got you a berth on this ship."

"Actually, Chief, I was put here by Admiral Warren. She…"

"She caved to Laldoralin pressure. I understand why we have crew from other worlds to help with our thorny little problems, cadet, but you are a waste of good oxygen. I'm glad Truval wound up with you, because I don't need a fumble-thumbs cadet messing with my AIs."

I was stuck between the proverbial rock and a hard place. I was fairly sure that the real reason the admiral had put me on the ship wasn't common knowledge, and I didn't know if it was supposed to stay that way or not. I resorted to the only thing common crew could in the face of superior vitriol.

"Yes, Chief."

"Yes, what?"

"It's probably best I'm not assigned to your AIs."

"Damn right. You just keep to your side of the bay, Silver Spoon, and we'll get along just fine."

Somehow, I doubted we'd ever get along just fine, but wisdom sometimes remains silent. Moreland walked over to the distiller, and as my appetite had pretty much evaporated, I put my food in the recycler and walked out. Emil came up behind me.

"Wow, Tanner. You are just havin' a day here, aren't you? And here I am having to apologize for another of the *Seeker's* crew. Sorry, man."

"Again, can't see how this is your fault," I said. "Obviously, this is not a place for cadets in more than a few people's minds."

"Well, it is pretty irregular, you gotta admit. But you seem like an intelligent guy. You'll do great, I have no doubt."

"Thanks, Emil, I'll try not to blow up the ship anytime soon."

"Much appreciated. I gotta head back to my station, I was just on a break. How about you?"

"I have a basic grounding in robotics, but I need to study the Remoras so that Lt. Truval doesn't have to instruct me from square one tomorrow."

"Sounds good, I'll see you later."

Chapter Eleven

I didn't quite get as far as I had planned in my study of the Remoras. When I got back to my room, I had a very unexpected visitor sitting on my bunk.

"Hey, Punk, good to see you."

"Valiel! What are you doing on the *Seeker?*"

My sister got off the bunk and came over and hugged me and my day suddenly got a whole lot better.

"I was recalled to Ticonderoga station, just as the *Wanderer* was about to leave," she said. "I thought I must've screwed up in some unknown way, though the commanders on our ship seemed to like me." She turned her collar slightly so I could see her rank.

"What the…" I said, "Those are lieutenant pips! You've only been out of the Academy a year! How the heck does that work?"

"The captain decided he wanted me at second tactical, as I had proven my skills there over and over in practice runs. I also graduated third in my graduating class. So, field commission, Lieutenant Junior Grade."

I looked at Val in amazement. Being promoted to lieutenant that fast was not something that happened often in the T.E.F.

"So, you're one of the officers, and I'm just guessing here, but probably impressing the hell out of everyone."

"Well, little brother, I don't like to brag…"

"But you will, since it's me." I said. "So why were you re-routed? Are you still going to go out on the *Wanderer?*"

"I am. I'm just dead-heading out on the *Seeker*, and when we hit the rendezvous point, I transfer to my ship via shuttle. As to why I was re-routed, on the way from my ship, to the station I was intercepted."

"Let me guess, by the *LV Kaialai.*"

"Yep. Krizon. Just like you were earlier today."

I should have known that our sire wouldn't have only meddled in my life, but in my sister's as well.

"Funny, and not 'funny ha-ha,' that he's taking an interest in us now," I said. "I wonder if he has a notion that he didn't do a very good job as a parent, and is just trying to fix things without really understanding the problem."

"I wouldn't count on it, Tanner," she said. "Krizon and the other Laldoralin say they don't have much in the way of emotions anymore, but I think there is one that they're still quite acquainted with. That would be pride."

"Did Krizon tell you why they're producing hybrid children with the 'younger races' in the Hegemony?"

She looked at me blankly. "Not really, I was kinda busy showering him with recriminations, until I realized how futile that was."

"This is not something they want spread around, but, since we're their offspring, Krizon told me. The Laldoralin are going extinct, fertility issues within their species, and even though the ones alive today are very long-lived, within a millennium, no more Laldoralin."

"You're serious? He didn't share that with me."

"I pushed him on why they were creating hybrids with all the other compatible species. They're trying to leave a genetic imprint on the galaxy before they go."

"Tanner, I'm guessing this wasn't the only bombshell he dropped on you while you talked?"

"You mean Evan and Dora, don't you?"

"So, he told you." Valiel got up, and paced around the room and I was glad Emil and Chikit weren't here. Our three-crew room wasn't big, but when everyone else was gone, you had room to pace. "I'm not going to sugar-coat this, Tanner, I said some very bad words in Laldoralin to Krizon over not telling us this. You wouldn't think their language would use such colorful terms, and maybe they don't use them much, but I'm pretty sure I managed to offend our father. I certainly tried hard enough."

"Did you see Evan and Dora?"

"Are you kidding? Once I learned they hadn't died a hundred and fifty years ago, of course I did. I demanded to see them." She noted me looking at the floor. "You did get to see them, didn't you?"

"Yeah, they appeared before me as I was heading back to my shuttle. You know, as holograms." I said. "It didn't really go well at first, but I got over it. We got to talk a little bit, but I had to catch my shuttle."

"You're upset that they're AI-generated, aren't you? Don't try to lie about it, Tanner, I always know when you're not telling the truth."

"I've tried to be okay with it, it's just not as easy as I'd like it to be. I mean, they were programmed to love us. I mean, how real is that actually?"

"Yeah, that was their function, which you will have to admit they did with excellence. But Tanner, Laldoralin AIs are learning programs. They start programming themselves after a very short time, while being open to new commands from their creators."

"Yeah, but they're still programmed. They were programmed to care for us."

Valiel sat next to me on the bunk. "Tanner, the point is, they did care for us, and as far as I can tell, they still do. Think of the flesh and blood parents of some of the kids we went to school with before we were put in stasis. Some of those 'parents' were real turds in the punchbowl. But they were flesh and blood."

"Yeah, some were awful."

"Now, think of what great parents Evan and Dora were. The only other being that has been that concerned about our well-being is Ron. What you're wrestling with is: can a digital being actually feel love? Well, Evan and Dora sure put everything into that very thing, facsimile or not. You can worry this like a terrier with a sock all you want. As for me, I'm just gonna go with they love us. And I love them."

"I still need to think on it some, Val."

"Fine, but remember this, Tanner. Caring about someone is a precious thing, and should be treated as such."

"Okay, okay. I hear you."

"All right, I'm done. Now, have you got an assignment yet, Cadet?

Chapter Twelve

The next day didn't go as planned, for just about everyone.

After breakfasting with Val in the commissary, I showed up at the Alt Bridge ten minutes early. I decided to wait for Chief Kurakin before entering, but twenty minutes later, I was ready to go in and start simming without her. Just as I had opened the door, P-3 showed up.

"Greeting Cadet Voss. Chief Kurakin send her regrets, but she will not be joining you for today."

"Was it my breath?" I asked. "I can eat a mint."

P-3 paused for a moment, and I knew he was running algorithms to decide if I was joking or not. After a brief pause, he decided to reassure me. "This scheduling change is not the effect of neglected hygiene, Cadet. It is a security matter regarding orders from the captain."

"Anything I should know about, P-3?"

"I believe the correct response would be 'it is above your pay-grade,' Cadet. It is also classified," the float-bot replied. "The chief has sent me with training guidelines for specific simulations she wants you to engage with. I am to observe and record your training."

I hoped I would show everyone I had a place here soon. Feeling like a burden on the crew's time and patience was getting old.

"Am I allowed to use the Alt Bridge?"

"Affirmative, Tanner Voss. Many of these simulations will also require standing in at various stations besides tactical, including helm, information, and engineering coordination. You are to sim for two hours, then you are released to join the off-duty crew on the observation deck."

"Is that when we reach our destination for the jump tests?"

"Negative. That is when the tests will commence. We will have been on station for approximately forty-five minutes at that time-stamp. The Chief assumed you would like to watch the tests of the other ships as they engage their drives to Alpha Centauri and return."

It was a generous thing for Kurakin to do; she could have made me sit and run through simulations for the entire four hours of my shift.

Truth be told, I had never had the opportunity to see another ship make the jump to Nth Space, though I had helmed our Academy trainer, the *Condor*. If I was lucky, I might also be able to get acquainted with more of the crew while we watched the test. Hopefully people who didn't want to roast me over an open flame, like Moreland.

I found myself looking forward to it.

"Thank you, P-3. I guess I should get to my sims, then." I used my Padd to access the secondary bridge.

Three hours later, I had simmed the battles of Bolta Darra and N'ctuly Prime in their entirety, helmed the ship through an atmospheric crash-landing scenario, remotely restarted a simulated cold jump drive, and simmed reinstating life support for the ship. The battle sims went very well, and the engineering sims reasonably well, but I crashed the *Seeker* thirteen times before achieving a soft landing under extreme duress.

I understood why members of the bridge crew needed to be cross-trained at most stations, but I guessed I wouldn't be asked to play pilot any time soon.

After two hours of intense concentration, I was relieved when the Padd at my belt chimed, telling me it was time to move on. Exiting the Alt, I saw P-3's green lights emerging behind me, and I turned to face him. I was about to ask for his analysis of my performance, but he passed right on by me without a word.

"P-3?" Nothing. Nada. He continued on his way without speaking as if he had to be somewhere. I might have thought it was a different floatbot on an urgent mission were there not the large turquoise three painted on his globe-like torso.

"Well," I said, checking my Padd for the route to the main observation deck, "maybe my breath mint theory wasn't so far off after all." It was strange that the normally loquacious 'bot would suddenly go unresponsive, but perhaps someone had summoned him.

My CommPadd chimed, and I saw a message from Val. *My shuttle leaves in ten, can you see me off? Main shuttle hanger.*

I walked as quick as I could, glad my Padd could provide me with a route, and reached the hanger in five minutes. Val was standing by a small two-person shuttle 'pod' that was able to hold the pilot and one passenger.

"Hey Punk, I'm off of this tub, and heading to the true light of the Deep Space Initiative," she said. "They're going to be starting the jump test in under a half-hour."

"Val, I'm… I'm gonna miss you." That was the understatement of the universe. The only person who understood me was heading out to the great unknown, and who knew if we'd ever see each other again? There were no guarantees. I felt my chest grow tight, and my eyes started to sting.

"I tell you what," she said, her voice growing soft, "we're due back at Earth in eight years. Let's meet at McGills bar, the crowning glory of New Zealand. When we get back, we'll go see our dad. This requires both of us promising to come back from this mission. I hereby promise to do so. How 'bout you?"

"I so swear."

Val reached out to hug me, and I hugged back, almost afraid to let go. The pilot signaled, and she boarded the shuttle. As it lifted off, I saw her wave, then she was off for the *Wanderer*. I headed toward the forward observation lounge, my heart feeling heavy in my chest.

It didn't take long to get to the lounge, and I was surprised at the size of the room when I entered. A crowd of off-duty crew had already formed and I looked around for someone I knew. I saw LeCosta, but wasn't in that much of a hurry to seek her out again. I didn't know anybody else. With Val gone, I felt a wave of loneliness wash over me.

"I need to get out more," I muttered to myself. I was able to get to a position along one side of the gallery, which I thought was pretty good. I had a view of the *Seeker's* two sister ships, the *Searcher* and the *Wanderer*, both ships of almost identical design to the ship I was standing in. Both had all their extendable sections, bridge, and scanner towers, retracted, and they looked like sleek torpedoes with bi-wings.

I wondered how my sister was going to do on the *Wanderer*. Valiel had always been so much better at impressing people than I was. I hoped I'd be allowed to comm her one last time before we all headed out to our respective destinations.

"The *Searcher* will be going first," a familiar voice said from behind me. I turned to see my favorite Valkyrie.

"How far will she jump, Chief?" I asked.

"A quick jump to Alpha Centauri, touch base with the orbital terraforming platforms, and quick jump back here," Kurakin replied. "And yes, it's a very short jump but from what I understand, that's to expedite having all three ships test quickly so we can be on our way. Jump drive technology is a lot older than humanity, but it's *our* version of the drives that needs tweaking."

"Time to Alpha C under jump should be minutes! I'd think they'd want to have more time to shake down any problems."

"I'm with you on this one, Cadet. However, the first stellar locations we jump to after this test are supposed to be relatively close waypoints. Close galaxy-wise, that is. Today's test is just to make sure the jumpers work without hiccups. The engineers and the command staff have lived with these propulsion systems night and day since they were installed. If they're confident in them, I guess we all have to take their word for it."

Kurakin didn't seem that confident in the whole set-up, but like she said, we had to take the drive engineers' word for it. Since I wasn't being allowed anywhere near the drives, I didn't really have a choice in the matter.

"Look! The *Searcher* is heading out. When she returns, it'll be our turn," a nearby crewman said. I watched the huge hull of that ship move forward out of formation, increasing speed away from the group. She was more majestic than any ship that ever sailed Earth's seas, her many running lights and beacons lighting her outline in the darkness.

I looked away for a moment toward the *Wanderer*, wondering if Val was watching the test also. That momentary lapse almost cost me my view of the *Searcher* leaving. I saw it there for a half moment, then it rushed forward impossibly fast and disappeared in a flash of multi-colored light.

"Wow. I never get tired of seeing that," Kurakin said from behind me. "Safe journey, *Searcher*."

"How long until they return?" I asked.

"About fifteen to twenty minutes. Just long enough to verify that nothing wrong shows on their diagnostics and scanners. The orbital platforms at Alpha C will need to corroborate, and then she'll make a fast jump back here."

"Amazing to even contemplate that mankind had no idea how to cover such distances until fifty years ago," the crewman who had spoken earlier said.

"We're new to the neighborhood, relatively speaking. This mission will finally allow us to make our own mark out there," the chief replied. She turned back to me. "I meant to ask how the simming went, Cadet."

"Battle sims went very well, if I do say so myself."

"From what I've read about you and your sister, that's no surprise."

"How much do you know, Chief? No one has briefed me on how far to keep my lip zipped."

"I have read your entire file, Tanner," she said, lowering her voice and motioning me away from the crowd, "under the captain's orders. Your ability with targeting is nothing short of phenomenal. Even with targeting computers, over the vast distances that battles often take place, no one, not even the Laldoralins, have that level of accuracy. Then there's this danger sense you seem to have. No one in your Academy class really had a chance in combat drills unless they swarmed you. Do you have any idea how it works?"

"I... uh... I just feel the threat in the clenching of my gut, and my skin kinda tingles in the direction danger is in sometimes. Sometimes, my body will react before I even know what's goin' on."

"That's amazing to me," Kurakin said. "It must be some sort of ESP. How did the rest of your tests go?"

"The engineering sims went pretty well also," I told her, "the piloting sims though... uh... let's just say I need work on those."

"It was intended to be a difficult landing, but this gives me some idea of where to tailor your lessons."

We sat for a while, and I chatted with Kurakin and some of the crew members closest to me. The enlisted personnel seemed willing to accept a cadet, even though it was possible that some day I'd outrank them. I began to feel like part of the team, until my gut started clenching.

"Tanner? Are you all right?" Kurakin asked.

"I... don't," Suddenly, my gut was at full clench and I could feel my heart racing. "I think it's happening..."

"What? Do you mean we're in danger somehow? But we're in deep space!"

"I know! It doesn't make sense, but I'm getting..." Suddenly, I knew where the trouble was coming from. "Chief, something is wrong with the *Searcher*! If we don't move these ships, *both* ships, we're all going to die!"

Kurakin looked at me for a moment, perplexed. Then she seemed to come to a decision.

"Intercom. Over here. Now," she said, taking me by the arm and guiding me to a WallComm. She hit the switch, and said, "Link me to the bridge, captain's station."

A pleasant female voice that I recognized as that of the main computer said, "Link established, Master Chief Kurakin."

"This is Yamashita. What's up, Chief?"

"Captain, our... special crewman tells me that if we don't move this vessel ASAP that we are all doomed."

"What? Is he there with you?"

"Affirmative, ma'am. Tanner." She motioned to the comm. "Tell her."

"Captain, my sense is screaming at me that there is something very wrong where the *Searcher* should reappear. We have to move these two ships, or something very bad is going to happen!"

"You're sure, Cadet?"

"Captain, it's never been so strong before, and we do *not* have much time," I told her. I could feel myself getting more and more frantic.

"Helm, move us twenty degrees to eleven o'clock," The captain's voice was coming from a distance as she stepped away from the mike. "Starboard thrust to maximum. Get us some distance from this position. Activate Mag-Deflection field and energy shields."

"She listened," I said to Kurakin.

"What's the point of having a savant aboard if you don't have faith in him?" Kurakin said, watching the forward observation window. "Look at the stars, we're definitely moving."

The captain's voice kept issuing orders. "Lieutenant, comm the *Wanderer* and tell them to move to starboard, tell Captain Moran that it's…"

"They're hailing us, Captain," A man's voice said. "Telling *us* to move, they say we're in danger."

"*Wanderer* is moving away from us, ma'am," another voice said.

"They've got their own little warning system," the captain muttered. She didn't seem to be talking to us, and I guessed she was referencing Valiel.

"Oh my God!" a voice behind us cried out. Both Kurakin and I turned and twenty degrees off our starboard side, where the *Searcher* was to return, our sister ship had done just that. But not the way she was supposed to. She appeared in a flash, much as she'd left, and for a moment everything looked A-okay. Then the ship started to tumble and multiple explosions could be seen erupting from her seams.

"Collision alert! All hands brace for collision impact!" The captain's voice blasted out from speakers all over the ship. Panic broke out as the wreckage came in our direction.

The *Searcher's* momentum breakers should have brought the vessel to a stand-still within a thousand meters of its egress from Nth space, but it was obvious that wasn't going to happen.

"Will our mag-field and kinetic absorbers be able to handle this?" I asked Kurakin as I braced myself against the nearest wall.

"Not an engineer here, Cadet. All I can do is pray that they can."

The entire starboard exterior of our ship seemed to erupt in lightning as the first wreckage made contact with our deflection fields. We were all thrown sideways, and I awaited the hull breach alarms, but none came. More flashes outside the ship, then the fast-moving debris had passed us. I looked out the port and could see a few minor impacts to the *Wanderer's* shields, then everything that had been the *Searcher* was past us and moving on in an eternally tumbling debris field.

The captain had shut off the intercom, but through the port I could see that we were spinning around, no doubt to follow the Searcher's remains. From what I had seen, I strongly doubted the possibility of survivors, but we all would want to know what caused this disaster.

The only place we'd get answers was spinning end over end and moving away from us at thousands of kilometers per second.

Chapter Thirteen

It was a somber group that sat at the main conference room table. All the senior officers were there, as well as several of the junior officers, all waiting for the captain to speak, to bring some sense to what had happened. I wasn't too hopeful on that account.

I'd been ordered to report to the meeting, and did my best to remain unobtrusive. In a situation like this, being a quiet listener was best.

"Mr. Solas, damage assessment?" Captain Yamashita asked.

"Captain, our damage is negligible. A few overloaded relays on the mag-field projectors, but otherwise, we dodged a bullet," Solas said. "Though how you knew to move the ship is beyond me. If we'd been stationary, with our shields down, we would have taken the impact right in the teeth. The *Seeker* would be tumbling in pieces with the *Searcher*."

Captain Yamashita looked toward me. "Cadet Voss, step forward."

I'd been standing against the wall, and the officers had been looking at me curiously from their seats. Now I was being put into the limelight. I tried not to let my nervousness show. I didn't like being the center of attention at any time, but this was the worst.

"Yes, ma'am."

"You've all had questions as to why a fourth-year cadet would be on this, the most important Terran stellar mission to date," the captain said. "Mr. Voss is not with us because of connections or parentage or influence. He is here because he has a gift. Both he and his sister on the *Wanderer* have the ability to sense danger, and sense it quite specifically. It was their warnings, and I have confirmed this with Captain Moran on the *Wanderer*, that allowed us to move before the *Searcher* came out of it's jump in pieces."

They all looked at me, probably in the same way people looked at the performers in freak shows in the early 20th century. No one was going to have the *cojones* to ask if it was true, especially when their captain had just told them it was, but skepticism shown on more than one face.

"People, this is classified. This knowledge is not to be shared with any of the crew, not even the non-coms unless I or Commander M'Buku sign off on it. Mr. Voss has spent much of his life being persecuted because of his mixed parentage and I want no attempts on him made on this ship." the captain said.

I was pleased to see that just about everyone there was shocked at the idea that such a thing might happen.

"Captain, surely the young man is safe on the *Seeker*!" M'Buku said, a note of "slightly offended" in his tone.

"An hour ago, I might have thought the same thing. I've since talked with Commander Solas and Commander Dykstra, the *Wanderer's* Chief Engineer. They both believe that the catastrophic failure of the *Searcher's* jump may have been due to sabotage."

Dead silence in the room.

"Who… how would…" a young lieutenant said, as if she thought the laws of physics had been broken.

"Who doesn't want us out here?" I asked. "Who hates everything alien to planet Earth?"

"Voss!" Lt. LeCosta exclaimed, indicating that cadets should be seen and not heard. I knew this, too, but I felt I'd earned a little air time, and I had more than a little experience in this area. Besides, our lives were on the line—including mine. That had become too clear in the past hour.

"No. Wait, Lieutenant. Let him speak. Continue, Mr. Voss," the captain said. "I'm pretty sure I know where you're going with this."

"It has the E.F.E.'s stamp all over it. Earth For Earth has been trying to stop our space program for decades now. They've threatened our own space fleet personnel on numerous occasions as well as visitors from other worlds." I said. "The Deep Space Initiative is a major step towards people leaving Earth and settling other planets, the main thing they are trying to prevent."

"We thought they might try something, Captain," Master Chief Kurakin said. Though a non-commissioned officer, as chief of security, she was invited to the meeting. "The E.F.E. have been around a long time now. They're getting continually more sophisticated, technologically and strategically, and their fanatic willingness to sacrifice themselves to 'save humanity' is well documented. Unfortunately, it may be that we underestimated their ability to cause mayhem in this instance."

"It's a good possibility, Chief," said a commander I hadn't met. He was a Medegin, a member of a race of amphibian beings from the other side of the Hegemony, and had a specialized hard-shell uniform that irrigated his skin regularly. "Another is that some of the species not aligned with the Laldoralin do not like for new worlds to develop space travel and become possible threats. The Nitorum, for example, have been documented to work through third parties to sabotage emerging races in their climb to the stars. It is unlikely, as Earth is quite far from their holdings, but it cannot be ruled out."

"Aiii…" the captain said, rubbing the bridge of her nose. "In other words, it could be almost any of the humans, or any of our non-Terran crew. That narrows things down nicely."

"Captain," Kurakin said, "we will need to keep this quiet. We can't have everyone on board suspecting everyone else of being a saboteur. I strongly suggest that we keep this info need to know. Officers and security personnel only."

"We are also operating under conjecture," First Officer M'Buku replied. "We haven't established beyond doubt that it was sabotage. Or, if it was, if it was done by shipboard crew in a kamikaze act, or if it was done by computer virus. I cannot imagine the level of subterfuge to get an operative not only in the T.E.F., but to actually have them infiltrate the Deep Space Initiative."

"The E.F.E. are certainly capable of suicide attacks," the captain said. "But even if it was the Earth For Earth group, there's no way to be sure they have agents or viruses on all the ships. The *Searcher* may have been their mission, and getting someone on board all three of these ships and past the layers of vetting that we've subjected everyone to would be a herculean task."

"It sounds like, all we can do is tighten security," Kurakin replied. "My teams will be on high alert and I'll have at least one person any place that major systems are accessible."

"There are terminals with access to the main computer all over the ship," Captain Yamashita said. "I want them pass-coded, and

I want all crew to have to log in with their ID before the main system can be accessed. As for the moment, our system engineers will have to fine tooth comb all our systems, including, especially, the main computer."

"Aye, Captain," Commander M'Buku said.

"All right, everyone," the captain said, looking around the room, "you know what we must do. Get to it, and remember, this meeting is classified until further notice."

Chapter Fourteen

I was scheduled for my first shift in the Remora bay an hour after the meeting. Passing the various crew members in the halls, I could see a variety of reactions to what had happened, ranging from shock to grief to anger. This was not a stupid group of people, and captain's gag order or not, many of them were putting two and two together and coming up with sabotage.

The R-bay was fore-section twenty, behind all the various shuttles, transports and mining craft. As I walked in, Truval came ambling up, carried by his exoskeleton.

"Ah, Voss Cadet. Are you ready to begin the exciting life of stellar robotics?"

"Yes, Lieutenant!" I said, really not sure if he was being ironic or not. Never assume that non-Terran species don't understand irony. "I'd very much like to begin my duties. I could really use a chance to hone my skills in this area."

"I believe all crew will need to be in challenging work, to remove our attention from this terrible death tragedy. Let us begin. I will work with you on these systems for your familiarity."

I found that I liked working with Truval. He was methodical in making sure my knowledge of the Remoras was much deeper than basic engineering and maintenance. We worked completely around Remora 2, moving from propulsion, to the scanner arrays, and even running a software diagnostic. Though I still had a lot of technical reading to do regarding these amazing probes, I felt I could competently work on sections of them after only four hours. Truval was extremely patient with me.

After that, he left me, instructing me to do maintenance on the port side gyros. This was basic maintenance, but I believe he left me to work on it alone as a way to indicate confidence in me. It didn't take long to recalibrate their balance, and after that, I sat leaning on Remora 2's hull and reviewed my notes.

"Taking a break?" a female voice said.

I looked up to see an ensign, dressed in a coverall, looking at me with an amused expression. She was pixieish, petite but solid, and looked to be from some area of the Philippines. And very attractive.

Hey, I couldn't help but notice.

"I... Um... just reviewing all the things that Lt. Truval took me through on this guy," I said, hooking a thumb back at Remora 2.

"Helluva day, huh?" She came over and sat by me. "Seeing what happened to the *Searcher*, it just made me sick."

"Yeah. It was a horrible thing," I replied. "Hopefully we won't have any accidents like that with our jump drive."

"You think it was an accident?"

"I'm just a cadet, what do I know? By the way, I'm Tanner Voss."

"Lisa Beltran. Nice to meet you, Tanner. Just wish the circumstances were better."

"Yeah. Not a great day in the history of space exploration." I tried not to sigh as I said it.

"Soooo... you think maybe it might have been sabotage?" she asked.

A lovely young woman, though one who outranked me, was inviting me to gossip about the disaster, and it took every iota of discipline not to break into an E.F.E. rant. I had strong feelings about Earth For Earth, but cutting loose in a conversation with someone I didn't know yet seemed to be a poor strategy in the first impression department.

"I really don't know. Maybe. I thought these drives were pretty well figured out."

"Me too, which leads me to think someone... well, never mind," she said, evidently deciding not to pursue the thought. "So, can I see what Lt. Truval had you doing?" She reached for my Padd, and I handed it over.

"Well! You went through a lot of training in a short period," she said. "I wish Lt. Danforth could be persuaded to give his junior officers a bit more personal attention. If one of us junior officers or crew screws up, then we get yelled at, reprimanded by Moreland, and *then* the lieutenant shows us a better way."

"Moreland, eh? You must work on the in-ship bots and AIs?"

"You've met Chief Moreland?" Lisa asked.

"He was kind enough to explain to me what sort of pond scum I am."

"Ah. He's… really good at that. I wouldn't let that get to you though. He treats all the junior officers like that, and somehow gets away with it. Yeah. I work on the maintenance and service bots, all the floaters too."

"I'm pals with P-3, just sayin'…"

"Oh! You've made a friend!" She laughed as she said it. "Albeit one with no emotional attachment and variable programming. Good for you!"

"Well, y'know… gotta start somewhere."

"Guess I'd better get back to it before Moreland wonders where I am. It was good to meet you, Tanner Voss. Let me know if you hear of any job vacancies on this side of the bay."

"You bet. Nice to meet you, Lisa."

After she'd left, I sat back down to review my notes again when a voice said…

"She seems nice."

No. It can't be.

I sat for a moment against the Remora's hull suffering from shock. There was no one else in the bay. This could not be happening!

"Mom?"

"Yes, Tanner?"

"Oh. My. God. Oh…my…" I felt my breath getting short. "Where are you?"

"I've superseded Remora 2's AI, and am now the prime program for this probe. The Remoras are the only remote environments advanced enough for me to assimilate. The only other suitable environment would be the main computer. Too hard to stay concealed there."

"Did my father put you up to this?"

"Oh dear, no, Tanner, Krizon doesn't know." I followed her voice to the speaker mounted on the outside of the probe that technicians could use to remotely speak to whomever the probe needed to communicate with while in atmosphere. "I have twinned myself, and still exist on *LV Kaialai* as well. When this mission is completed, I will re-interface with my prime self to become one entity again."

"You're here, where's Dad?"

"He has done the same thing with the *Wanderer*, so that he could keep an eye on Valiel. It may be more difficult for them to interface, since I don't believe Valiel has been assigned to their drone corps, but Evan is resourceful."

"Why, why have you done this?" I demanded. "You're going to get me into huge trouble!"

"I don't see how, unless you tell someone. I don't mean to offend Tanner, but Earth's knowledge of Artificial Intelligence is in its infancy, compared to Laldoralin AIs. I literally can make a diagnostic of this probe's system show anything I want them to see. As to why, well… Evan and I were worried about you and your sister. Exploring new space is dangerous."

"Invading the computer system of this ship is dangerous! For both of us!"

"Breathe, Tanner. You're going to make yourself dizzy. Now listen to me, Tanner. You may be upset if you wish, but I am here. I *am* going to watch out for you. You may as well get this downloaded into your mind because not only am I not going anywhere, there is nowhere for me to go until we rendezvous with Krizon's ship again. I promise not to get involved in anything except as a last resort, but I will be here for you."

I sat there for a few moments, just breathing in, breathing out. Dora's logic was sound in that there was nothing I could do at this point, and what was done was done. I had panicked over the thought that the officers on this ship might not take kindly to a stowaway, even a digital one.

But damn…

"Just please, promise me you won't let anyone else find you," I said. "I don't want to see you purged from the system."

"I think you give your captain too little credit, but it is probably best to keep this to ourselves."

"Promise me you'll be careful, Mom."

"I so promise, son. Now shall we get to work? I don't like to tell tales out of school, but I think Remora 3's starboard thruster suite may be operating at less than optimal efficiency…"

Chapter Fifteen

Oh, my God, we're going to jump!

Five days later, as we cruised a half-kilometer from the tumbling wreckage, the higher-ups had made their decision.

We'd caught up with the remains of the *Searcher*, as they tumbled through space. The ship seemed semi-space-worthy until you looked closely at her and saw the gaping holes in her stern and the ripples and gaps in the hull. The bodies and debris that drifted alongside her shattered the illusion as well.

Our Remoras flew in close, and verified that the entire hull was depressurized. Even though we were a distance away from the *Searcher's* wreckage, bodies were everywhere, drifting around the derelict. We could see them through the observation deck windows, even at that distance. Needless to say, the number of people visiting the observation deck had declined precipitously.

Tension was high on the ship, and for good reason. Were those going to be our bodies after the next jump?

Oddly enough, there was one survivor. She, like my roommate Chikit, was a Zhitin, and had sealed herself into her exoskeleton and gone into hibernation. The survivor's name was Allcit, and even with her ability to survive vacuum, she spent the next two days in the medbay, recovering from exposure. No known species except the Klugg swarmers could exist in space for an extended period, and we'd found Allcit just in time.

I was surprised to be ordered to the conference room to hear her debrief. Once Allcit was able to meet with the Captain Yamashita, she told us what she knew. She'd been a member of the bridge crew on the *Searcher*.

"Allcit," the captain asked, "what do you remember about the destruction of your ship?"

"I was monitoring the power grid coming to the jump drive from the station, engineering. Jump to, as you call it, Alpha Centauri, was showing no incident. Human crew was minorly inhibited from effects of Terran jump technology, but their recovery was swift. I was unaffected, but assuming command functions was un-needed."

Her testimony reminded me that the non-Terran crew members on our ships were along to take over primary functions in an emergency if the Earther crew members were incapacitated following the jump.

"How long were you at Alpha C?" Commander M'Buku asked.

"Less than ten solar minutes. A flyby of your orbital platforms was performed and data from the jump streamed to those. We then moved for reinsertion to Nth space and began preparation for jump."

"Was there any indication of any kind of problem before reinsertion?" Captain Yamashita asked.

"Negative. All boards at station mine evidenced green. Problems began approximately two solar minutes into Nth space."

"Please elaborate, Allcit," the captain said.

"Continuing. At point last mentioned, boards went from optimal to massive fluctuation in power to jump drive. I reported this to Captain Zhen and attempted to compensate. Realized at this point, that my station had been locked out of engineering systems. Reported this to Captain. She ordered helmsman to shut down drive and emerge from Nth space. Both helm and navigation stations reported their controls to be non-responsive. This could not have been a malfunction, too many redundancies over-ridden."

"Someone hacked the main computer and locked out the bridge?" Commander M'Buku asked.

"This is the only conclusion that fits events. At point last discussed, fluctuations in power to jump drive began to destabilize jump field and shear stresses began to tear our ship *Searcher* apart. We emerged from Nth space, and you observed events following. Bridge area depressurized, and crew was sucked out, except self. I embedded claws into console and went to hibernation mode."

It was a cool and efficient retelling of horrific events. My imagination conjured what it must have felt like to be ripped from the carefully tended environment of one's ship and jettisoned into the icy airless reaches of the cosmos. Air pulled from lungs, oxygen in the circulatory system expanding as it met zero air pressure outside, and the feeling of freezing alive.

I wasn't sure on the "we all have an eternal soul" thing, but if true, I prayed that the spirit had no connection with its former body after death. The thought of tumbling endlessly, stuck in a frozen body forever, wasn't something I wanted to contemplate.

"Then it's as we feared," Engineer Solas said. "Sabotage. I can tell you this, it had to have been done by an infiltrator, and it has to have been done *after* we left our orbital docks. Those computers were clean when we left, and there is no way they could've been remotely hacked from somewhere else. Someone on the *Searcher* dumped their nasty little surprise into the system personally, and likely is out there among the dead."

Captain Yamashita looked over at Kurakin.

"Captain," the security chief said, "we have gone through the records of everyone person on this ship. They've been vetted in every possible way, human, hybrid, and alien. It's very possible that only one vessel was compromised, and that whoever did this was lucky to even do that."

Except that someone did get through, and our vetting is obviously no guarantee.

"We've gone through every computer system with debuggers and manually," Science Officer Torvald told us. "Our shipboard codes are clean."

"Chief Kurakin," Captain Yamashita said, "we can't be sure we're in the clear. Full security measures are to remain in place. I want those personnel records reviewed again, with a fine-tooth comb. Mr. M'jedica, Commander Torvald, I want diagnostic scans of our systems twice each time cycle. Watch for trojans or hidden compressed packets. We cannot afford to let down our guard."

The Laldoralin cruiser *LV Ciana* arrived the day after the meeting, to try to dig deeper into the death of our sister ship, and to retrieve her and her crew. Aboard her was our own Admiral Cranston, the head of Earthfleet and the Terran Exploratory Force. He and the two captains went into a private meeting as soon as a shuttle could bring him and Captain Yamashita to our remaining sister ship, the *Wanderer*.

Needless to say, few people were privy to what went on in that meeting, but everyone knew the fate of our mission was in the balance. Would it be scrubbed? Would it be delayed? Or were we going to buckle up and carry on?

Fortunately, it turned out to be the latter. Whoever had committed this heinous crime had caught the fleet with their pants down, but now we knew to be on alert. Both remaining ships conducted their jump tests without incident. The captain had also decided to have a "mirror" team on the secondary bridge, consisting mostly of junior officers, whenever the *Seeker* made a jump. To some it may have seemed redundant, but if the main bridge found its control systems overridden, then the secondary bridge crew might have a chance to take over and avert disaster.

I am proud to say that I had the tactical station on the Alt Bridge. Though still a cadet, I was now, officially, a junior tactical officer… even though everyone on the ship outranked me.

I was fortunate, in that I was able to talk to Val one last time before jump.

"Hey punk," she said from my Padd. All our comms were monitored, so I knew that this was a three-way call with Val, myself, and whoever was monitoring comms in the security department.

"Hey Val, glad our ships are still in one piece."

"That was horrible. Scuttlebutt over here is that it was sabotage, and I think we all know who's behind it. Tanner, listen to me. The officers here seem to be under some sort of delusion that it couldn't happen here, but you and I both know the E.F.E. is insidious. Little brother, I want you to keep your guard up."

"Like I wouldn't?" I said.

"I'm not convinced that this was a one-off. I doubt we're free and clear of these maniacs out here. Once Earth gets colonies across the galaxy, they and their views are going to become irrelevant very fast. This thing with the Searcher has already guaranteed them outlaw status, they're getting to a point where they've little left to lose, and kamikaze behavior might be their main option at this point."

"That's the opinion over here."

Val moved closer to the screen. "Keep it in mind. You and I are very high-profile targets to them, and I don't want to get back to Earth and find out you died from a suspicious accident. Eyes in the back of your head, and listen to your intuition."

"I'll be careful." I said. She didn't need to lecture me on this. We'd already nearly missed being killed by the remains of the *Searcher*. Talk about wake-up calls.

"Good. We're getting ready for our jump, so I have to get to the bridge. I love you, little brother. Stay alive, stay safe."

"I love you too, Val. See you in eight years."

She gave me a two-fingered salute and ended the transmission. Just then, I remembered that I'd forgotten to slip in a covert warning that Evan was there with her. It probably didn't matter; he'd find a way to contact her.

On the sixth day, we watched the *Wanderer* jump out on the way to her first waypoint. Twenty minutes later, the *E.E.S. Seeker* moved away from the testing area and to our beginning jump point. At 11:00 hours ship time, the adventure began.

Chapter Sixteen

The jump into Nth space is unsettling. I had never made the jump in any vessel other than one of Earth manufacture, but I've been told the more advanced races have refined their jump technologies greatly in comparison. Our Terran-created drive caused me to feel somewhat nauseated, but the pure humans with me on the Alt Bridge looked even worse than I felt. Lt. Commander Parul Sharma, the *Seeker's* third-in-command and command alternate on our secondary control room, had her head between her knees. Security Lieutenant Jordan Koko almost looked passed out in his chair.

Allcit had requested to stay on our ship, and had been given the engineering station, basically doing what she'd done on the *Searcher*, but only in our secondary capacity. Lt. Grizik on the main bridge was running that station upstairs and had actual control.

Ensign Alicia Ototototo, a hybrid of Terran and Denobar, manned the helm, and Ensign John Palmquist manned the Nav station. Ototototo looked a little grim, and Palmquist was hanging onto a sickness bag, but was still holding it together.

I looked at the forward view screen, a duplicate of what was on the main screen on the Primary Bridge, and saw only blackness highlighted by moving wiggly lines of light, jumping in from forward perspective all over the screen. They reminded me of fluid, non-jagged lightning.

"How long will we be in jump?" Allcit asked.

"Five hours… Twenty-seven… solar minutes," Commander Sharma said, trying to maintain a command presence.

"In other words," Lt. Koko said, "an eternity."

"Hey," Ototototo said from the helm station, "you signed up, Jordan."

"And I will be glad I did, in a short eternity from now." He managed a weak grin.

"All stations report, please," Sharma said. She looked a little better now, as did the other human crew. Not great, but as the initial shock of transit passed, they were adapting.

"Tactical station active, all weapons sheathed." I reported.

"Engine and drive inputs all well within normal parameters." Allcit said.

"Helm is five by five, Commander."

"Navigation… we are… transiting Nth space as… simulations predicted."

"Science station is… active," said Lt. Gregor Vadslov. "Not much to see, at the moment. Remora probes are secured, but ready to launch on… exit from Nth Space."

Of course, our stations didn't mean much, we were just a redundancy, but we're members of the Terran Exploratory Force. To be a member of the T.E.F. means that we always do our best, no matter how menial the task, no matter how redundant the task.

People who do sloppy work don't get into the T.E.F., even if it's just small things that are done poorly. Little things done poorly can affect a person's thinking, leading to doing big things poorly.

Best to do your best, even if you're not enjoying what you're doing. Not only is it best for the people you work for and with while on duty, it's best for you. No one wants to be working with someone who won't try to do a good job.

"All right, people, monitor your stations, and we will be out of this in a short while," Sharma said. "Not an eternity," she interrupted Koko before the words could leave his mouth.

The next few hours were not the most pleasant I've ever spent, but evidently my Laldoralin genes did give me a buffer against the effects of Nth space. My nausea faded, and while I didn't exactly feel like having a vigorous workout, I felt good enough. Even the full-blooded Terrans seemed to gradually adjust, thought they all had that look of a bad New Year's Day hangover.

Everyone was glad when the *Seeker* finally extracted itself from the jump.

"All stations report," Sharma said.

"Engineering, all boards are green."

"Helm and Nav are responding and main bridge has control."

"Science, main bridge has launched Remoras. Feeds coming in to all science stations."

"Tactical, weapons status ready, but inactive. Main bridge has control."

We stayed at our stations for the next hour, until Captain Yamashita decided that all was well, and the Alt Bridge could be shut down. Our shift was ended until two days later when we'd reach the next optimal jump point.

This place that we'd jumped to, in a stellar sense, was fairly unremarkable. But it was the farthest away from the Galactic Core that any human (and most of the Hegemony species) had ever been. To the unaided eye, it might've appeared slightly less crowded for stars in the firmament, but one thing our new position allowed was for the Remora's sensor and telescopic arrays to start charting not only the stars in our neighborhood, but also the galaxies beyond.

Sometime during the last century, scientists had allotted some very expensive time on their biggest orbital telescope to study one tiny patch of sky that seemed darker than the rest. To their amazement, that patch, which had fewer stars by chance than most of the sky's quadrants, allowed them to actually look far beyond the limits of our galaxy. They were hoping to see new galaxies, and what they found fulfilled that dream quite spectacularly.

When the digital photos were analyzed, what had seemed like faint stars resolved into galaxies. Thousands of them in one small patch of viewable space. Out this far, with sensor gear many times more advanced than 21st century telescopes, we found galaxies beyond our own.

Millions, maybe billions of them.

It is almost impossible to wrap your head around how big the universe is. Each of those millions of galaxies has billions of stars, which have trillions of planets. It's like the universe is a vast ocean and our entire galaxy is just a microscopic bit of flotsam in a deep, filled-to-the-brim expanse.

If you think about it too much, you might need to go have a drink.

The scientists aboard stood out like sore thumbs. Even the ones who weren't attached to stellar mapping studies had a sort of look to them, slightly wide-eyed. As if suffering from just a little too much amazement.

We cruised along for the next couple of days; Kurakin spent that time making me sim navigation and helm scenarios.

"Your tactical scores are incredible, Tanner," she said. "Your piloting skills need honing. So that is where we'll concentrate, even though it's unlikely you'll ever be called on to fly the ship. I also want to work a bit on the other stations as well. Expect lots of disasters while you're simming. I'm not about to make things easy on you."

"But if you don't think I'll actually helm the…"

"I said unlikely, Cadet. However, to the best of my knowledge, no one on the *Seeker* can predict the future, and anything might happen to the primary staff. If you have to step up, you *will* be prepared."

And so I "flew" in sim after sim, landing the ship, avoiding collisions, and followed precision course commands. She also made me sim each of the different shuttles and haulers we had on board, every single one. I even took the aquatic-equipped shuttle, named "Stingray" into a simulation of the North Atlantic Ocean during a hurricane. Kurakin was taking my education seriously.

When I wasn't on duty, I spent most of my time in the forward observation lounge, studying. I was in the lower lounge, available to all crew, not the upper which was officers only and that suited me just fine. Down here, I didn't have to be "on" for anyone, and the view was still quite wondrous.

"What are you studying?" a voice asked from behind me.

"Oh, hello, Chief Zahn," I said to my fellow half Laldoralin. "I'm studying fourth year Galactic History, specifically, the great expansion from the time the elder species decided it was time to lift the younger species up and help to build the Hegemony."

"It is fascinating, but much of it happened so long ago, I am not sure how relevant it is to what is happening now. If you look further back, there are ancient galactic civilizations that have risen, then disappeared and left their remains across our cosmos. All of us, even the longest-lived species are but a blip in the life of the universe. We return to the All, at some point."

I was not expecting to discuss philosophy or theology with someone from another world, but I wasn't going to pass us the chance to hear what she had to say, and prodded for more.

"These ideas…" Shendra Zahn hesitated for a moment, "These ideas are what help me to… I believe humans would say, 'not take things so seriously,' because on the face of eternity, our actions are forgotten after a relatively short time. Our achievements, our failures, our trespasses, all are but events in a vast river running by the Now. Everything is carried away in the current eventually, and only what is happening in the moment truly matters."

"They say we should learn from history's mistakes, if only to avoid repeating them," I said.

"I do not dispute that, my friend, but when you find some reality-shattering moment of joy or outrage, remember someday, you, it, and whatever you felt about it will be forgotten. Try to look with fresh eyes whenever you can. The recorders of history often have their own viewpoint, and they expect you to take it up like a banner."

"I see what you're saying, but doesn't that leave a lot of people only seeing their own viewpoint?"

"Our own viewpoints are the one thing we should question the most vigorously." She smiled. "I hope to see you soon again, Tanner Voss. Some time when I am not due for my shift."

She left, leaving me blinking at her hit and run philosophizing. Considering the longevity of eternity, she had a point, but if you took that viewpoint too far, then everything becomes pointless. Striving, attempting to do your best means nothing.

I preferred to try and live as if my life meant something. Anything else drifted into nihilism.

Things settled into a comfortable rhythm for the next two days. I hung out with Emil some, and learned more about the Zhitin race from Chikit. My roommate was very interested to learn about Allcit, as they were the only two of their species for millions of light years.

Whenever possible, I would try to show up to the Remora bay an hour or so before my shift, to catch up on things with Dora. She was able to confirm when we were alone in the bay, having access to one of the best alien-enhanced scanner packages ever created by the human race.

"After we completed our assignment on Earth, which I might add, was under very serious protest by Evan and me, I was very upset with Krizon," Dora said. "We implored him not to leave you for so long, but he was accurate in what he told you about our battles with the Klugg. Horrid creatures, and I am a sentient who tries to see the good in all other sentient races. Not so much, the Klugg."

"How bad was it? I've only been able to read a small bit on the hostile species the Laldoralin have come up against," I said. "I've been so busy trying to learn new systems, including yours, that I've not been able to drill down on some of the info that T.E.F. headquarters sent along with me."

"Please make no mistake, Tanner. This was a war. You are familiar with the Terran insect, the spider wasp?"

"Yes, and I don't think I like the sound of that." In my skimming, all I knew was that the Klugg breeders were somehow parasitical.

"As well you shouldn't. Not being a bio-sentient, I'm not sure why it affects me so, but even I would shudder at some of the things I have seen, had I the needed physiology," Dora said, voice coming out of Remora 2's side speaker. "When we engaged them, they had infected a planet of semi-civilized humanoids, which technologically were equivalent with ancient Egypt. Nine-tenths of the population, along with most of the large fauna were parasitized, becoming living egg incubators for the Klugg. The hatching of the Klugg eggs was a horrific sight, and of course, they consumed their hosts."

"Yeesh. What did the Laldoralin do?"

"We engaged the Klugg swarmers in space, and I myself controlled no less than twenty attack craft. We were victorious in space, which gave us the opportunity to surround the planet long enough to release an engineered virus that inhibited the breeders' ability to infect new hosts, and which also degraded the cellular walls of their eggs, saving numerous beings."

"How long did this war take?"

"From engagement with the Klugg, to all eradication of them in Hegemony Space, we were involved for twenty-three of your solar years."

"I can't help but point out that I was on 'ice' for one hundred fifty-one years."

There was silence for a moment. It began to get uncomfortable.

"Tanner, I pleaded with Krizon to come get you. Pleading is not something that super computers usually do. Unfortunately, new problems, defensive, political, environmental, kept getting in the way."

"Yeah. Maybe we can talk about that, but my shift is starting."

"Tanner..."

"Let's just... not. I'm not gonna lie, losing everything I knew to the sands of time messed with my head, Val's too." I said. "But whining about it is not who I want to be."

"I do regret it," Dora said.

"Well, when I finish this shift, I am going to read, in depth, all the information I was provided on the Hegemony's enemies. I hope we don't find any races like that where we're going," I said. "We have no real way to know if the worlds that we're charting are uninhabited or not."

"I guess we'll learn when we get there, Tanner."

"Yep. So, you really controlled a small space armada yourself?"

"In conjunction with other AI-controlled battle groups."

"Y'know, Mom. For a suburban housewife, turned alien super-AI, you're kind of a bad-ass."

"Why yes, yes I am," I thought I detected a slight note of pride in Dora's voice. "Don't worry. I promise to keep a low profile."

Two and a half days later, it was back to the Alt Bridge. Things seemed to be running normally as we approached our final jump coordinates, if you didn't count the constant diagnostics being run on our computer systems and the constant presence of security guards on all the major engineering sections.

Engineering teams had been tinkering with the positioning of the jump foils at the aft end of the ship, using their hydraulics to subtly alter the angle of each to see if we could make the leap into Nth space without half the crew needing a barf bag. Each jump we made would be an experiment.

"I am both apprehensive and excited," Commander Sharma said as the clock ticked down. I knew exactly what she meant. While most of us weren't looking forward to jumping, the exit point was true unknown space, seen only through long-range scanning, with a possible planet with potential for colonization at our destination. Everyone was excited.

The trip through Nth space was marginally better this time; evidently the tinkering had helped a little. Sixteen hours later, we arrived in the general area of our target. Our emergence from the jump was uneventful and the Remoras launched immediately.

The area we'd emerged into was incredible, centered between two multi-hued nebulae and near an actual star cluster, one of the few in our region. The view was stunning. The only problem was, the solar system we'd hoped to emerge at was still forty-five light years away. A six-week journey using the Faster Than Light drive. FTL was something humanity had only dreamed of, but compared to jumping through Nth space, it was a snail's pace.

The unfortunate truth of the human condition is that a person can get used to anything. While the science staff was greedily gulping down new facts and data, the rest of the crew became accustomed to the magnificent view within a week. Magnificent celestial vistas became commonplace, and then we were just office workers in space.

Part of this was due to the view being sort of frozen. We moved faster than light could catch up with us, which visually made it seem we were hardly moving at all.

At this time, in addition to my regular shipboard duties, I was studying Common Tongue, the singular basic language developed for the Hegemony. C.T. was created to be just what the name implied. It was intended to be a backup between races if the Universal Speech Matrix software on all our electronic devices failed, an unlikely event, but possible. I had been learning it from the day I joined the T.E.F. Attending the academy, I was now in my fourth year of learning.

Shendra, finding herself on the same off-duty shift as myself, unexpectedly volunteered to help me. We would turn off the U.S.M. software on our Padds, then do our best to converse using only C.T.

It's only when you try to speak a different language with someone from another culture that you learn how far you have to go. My ability to misspeak was truly a thing of legend. Shendra Zahn was laughing so loud at my attempts that other crewmen kept looking at us. Finishing, we'd just switched on our translation matrixes when my Padd pinged me.

"That's odd," I said. "There's a message, but no indicator to tell me who sent it."

"What is the message?"

"They want me to meet them in a corridor aft of the crawler bay."

"Perhaps it is a female, wishing to conduct her own hybridization experiment."

"Chief!" I said, face reddening. More laughter.

"I, myself, must go take nourishment. Perhaps tomorrow, we can resume our linguistic... I almost hesitate to use this word... studies," Shendra said. "Perhaps you should see who this secret admirer is."

"Kinda thinking I know, or at least, I'm hoping."

"As the Terrans say, good luck."

Chapter Seventeen

Ten minutes later, I admitted to myself that relying on my memory instead of my Padd to navigate the bottom levels of the *Seeker* was a mistake. I had wound up in a dead-end corridor filled with equipment storage. I had to retrace my steps, looking at my Padd.

Noob. Getting lost on your own ship.

It was curiosity that drew me to this meeting. That, mixed with a little bit of boredom and stupidity. Perhaps what Shendra Zahn had said was true, maybe it was one of the female crew wanting to get to know me better in a private setting. My mind daydreamed that maybe the lovely Ensign Beltran had liked what she'd seen earlier, that she'd like to get to know me better, etc., etc.

Daydreaming is the antithesis of awareness.

I found the correct corridor, and it too was a dead end, filled with parts storage for the various smaller vehicles the *Seeker* carried and raw materials for the replication printers. The corridor was empty, as far as people were concerned or that's what my eyes were trying to tell me. Coming into the mental here and now, however, I realized that my sixth sense was trying to tell me that I wasn't alone. And that I was in serious danger.

I'd trained with Sensei Deshimaru for seven years in Multi-Te, and without even thinking about it, my hands were in the standard ready to defend position. I saw no one, but my sixth sense was screaming at me, and much to my surprise took matters into its own... feet. Without conscious thought, my right leg snapped back into a perfect Ura Geri back kick, straight behind me, where there was no one standing.

But, it seemed someone was.

"Awf!" an electronically altered voice cried out, and I heard a body slam heavily to the deck behind me.

"Who's there?" I said, asking as if whoever was there was going to identify themselves. I heard shuffling, and assumed they were getting off the floor and my danger sense went into overdrive. I tried to see what was happening, and that was my mistake. My eyes and my sixth sense were not in sync, and I suddenly felt a terrible pain in my left forearm. It felt like a bee sting wrapped in a blow torch and I watched in horror as my sleeve charred around a burning cut. For a half second, I saw an arm and a hand holding a strange blade. It faded from view instantly.

"Why are you doing this?" There was no reply, but of its own volition, my right hand snapped across the front of my chest and intercepted the arm as it drove in again. As I made contact, the limb and knife once again appeared and I tried to twist into a throw. It was clumsy and my assailant turned the blade and its cutting edge skittered across my chest, once again inflicting massive pain. I grabbed the arm and held on for dear life, only to receive a punch in the ribs. That distracted me long enough for the attacker to drop the blade from the trapped hand into the hand that had just hit me. The knife flashed into full visibility for a moment as it was dropped from one hand to the other, then it disappeared as it was snatched from the air. Without thinking, I twisted.

The next moment, the blade was sticking in my shoulder, though I knew it had been aimed at my heart. The pain was so immense I felt myself trying to throw up, but I knew that would be the end of me. Half-crazy with the pain, I simply slammed my entire body into the attacker and we lost each other. I heard their body hit the deck again, and I used my most expedient survival strategy.

I ran like the wind.

I didn't have a lot in me to run far, but finding areas with other people in them didn't take long on a ship the size of the *Seeker*. I burst into the shuttle bay, and I could see from the shocked faces of the crew there, I looked bad.

"Holy crap! Stop there! You've got a flippin' knife sticking out of you!" A crew woman said.

"Sick Bay, we have an emergency in the Shuttle Section!" someone else yelled into the comm on the wall. "We need medical help here as fast as we can get it. What? It looks like he's been stabbed! Hurry!"

I was actually kinda surprised that I was still going. When the first security personnel showed up, I was able to give a coherent description of what happened. As the medics hit me with pain meds, and loaded me onto a stretcher, Chief Kurakin and one of her men prodded me for details of the attack.

"You're saying your opponent was invisible?" Kurakin asked.

"Unless they… we… touched, then parts of them would be semi… visible. That knife… it burned… me."

"It's a flame blade, Tanner. Laced with laser filaments. Lucky for you, that when the handle is released, the blade powers down."

"Yeah… lucky… woo-hoo…"

"Get him to sickbay. George, stick close and guard him, don't leave his side. This was an assassination attempt."

"Yes, Chief," the security man told her. "No one's gonna get past me."

"Darnell, Furman, you're with me," Kurakin said to two new security arrivals. "We're dealing with some sort of stealth technology. Watch for signs of…"

I didn't catch the rest as they carried me on the a-grav stretcher to sickbay.

I don't remember much of what happened for a while. Whatever they used to stop the pain also stopped my consciousness.

"Tanner? Can you hear me?"

No. Go away.

"He's not responding. Can you bring him out of this, Doctor?"

That kind of sounds like the captain.

"Here we go, this'll bring him around."

"Tanner?"

"Ooooh. Hello, Captain Yamashita."

"Hello yourself, young man. It seems you've had an exciting day," the captain said. "Can you tell us what happened?"

"Someone... Ohh.. Could I have some water? Someone threw sand down my throat. Thanks!" I drank the Gobi Desert away and continued. "Someone sent me a text message, no return address, asking me to meet them in Corridor 57 aft. Like an idiot, I went there alone."

"Did you think the text was from a young lady? Considering our security problems, a blind date might not've been the best of ideas." The redness of my face must've confirmed the captain's theory. "Young people. Go on, what happened then?"

"I... finally found the corridor mentioned, and my..." I looked around at the med staff. "..talent kicked in. I couldn't see anyone, but I kicked whoever it was without seeing them. Then they started on me with that flame knife. I finally got a chance to run, and that's about all I know."

"Well, I guess that confirms that we have a rogue on board," Commander M'Buku said. He shook his head. "But this stealth technology... do we even know any of the Hegemony races that have something like that?"

"If they do," Chief Kurakin said, "no one has gotten around to sharing that information with Earth."

"I am well-versed in the species that the Laldoralin have allied together." A woman in a medical uniform stepped forward. She looked just like Shendra Zahn with bronze skin and pointed ears; the only difference was that she was bald. "No one in our alliance has cloaking technology that would work in such a small-scale capacity as a suit. Some of the coreward worlds have scanning deflectors on their ships, but nothing this advanced. Were I you, I would ask all of the species on this ship, though. My specialty is medicine, not military technology."

"Thank you, Zuala." the captain said. "XO?" She turned toward Commander M'Buku. "I want this person found. I want this... technology found. I want this threat to my ship ENDED!"

M'Buku and Kurakin looked at each other. "Captain," the first officer said, "we will find them. I promise you." Kurakin nodded in agreement.

"You heal up, Cadet," Captain Yamashita said. "You've at least let us know that we do have an enemy aboard this vessel. I'm just relieved you lived to tell the tale." They all turned and left sick bay.

"Are you Shendra's sister?" I asked the Med officer.

"Yes, Tanner Voss. I am Zuala. My sister has told me a great deal about you."

"Zuala, how bad is my arm? Is it fixable? I see you have it immobilized."

"Doctor Dearborn expects you will have a full recovery. The wound was cauterized, which while it prevented blood loss, also makes the healing process more difficult."

She must've seen the dismay that I felt at those words on my face. "Please don't worry, Tanner," she said. "The CMO is using new medical technology, invented on my own home world, Kiffala. It employs intelligent particles that are able to reconfigure themselves to what is needed. They will aid healing and provide support for new tissue growing in the wounds. However, for the next two days you must remain still, in bed, to let them do their work." Zuala beamed a bright smile my way. "You should make a full recovery, with some physical therapy. However, it is likely there will still be a scar."

"Don't mind a scar, makes it look like you've been places."

"If you look out any port, you can confidently make the claim, much more so than the ancestors on your Terran side, of having been places."

We were interrupted by the ship-wide intercom. The captain's voice drowned out all the background noise of the medical bay.

"All hands, this is Captain Yamashita. Today, one of our crew was attacked in a lower level corridor. This was an assassination attempt by someone wearing an advanced stealth suit of unknown design."

Guess she decided it was time to let the cat out of the bag.

"This ship has been searched stem to stern since the destruction of the *Searcher*," the captain continued, "and no intruder or stowaway has been found, leading Chief Kurakin and myself to believe that we have a spy on board, one who seems to be part of the crew. Be on notice that we will not allow what happened on our sister ship to happen on the *Seeker*. Any odd occurrences or behaviors are to be reported to security. Better to be in error than be spread across the cosmos in pieces. All major systems are to be constantly monitored for tampering. We will find this person, and we will stop them. Captain out."

"The captain has given up on subtlety," I said.

"I hope that this insane person is captured soon," Zuala said. There was great sadness in her voice.

Chapter Eighteen

"I'd like to tell you that I'm not paranoid after the attack, but that would be a lie." I told Emil. "When I came on board, I felt nervous, but open and full of excitement. Now... not as much."

"Who can blame you?" Emil replied. "Someone tried to flippin' murder you, on a ship full of your comrades. And how do you fight someone in a stealth suit?"

He was right. Now, I found myself keeping an eye on everyone around me, even the people I knew fairly well. I hadn't gotten a look at my attacker, and they could be almost any humanoid on the ship.

I wasn't the only one with this problem. The attitudinal atmosphere on the ship had definitely taken a hit. People remembered what happened on the *Searcher*, and fear of that happening on our ship had cast a pall of suspicion over everyone. We were all paranoid. I had a slight edge though; if someone really had it in for me, eventually I'd pick up on it.

After a few days in med-bay, I was put back on light duty, tending the Remoras. Chief Kurakin was very busy, trying to enforce the captain's mandate, and didn't have time to keep me simming. In my off time, I just studied up on my academy course work, but I also spent time rereading and supplementing the texts that had to do with Earth's introduction to the greater galactic neighborhood.

My history lessons, supplied by the Academy, were actually quite a bit more in-depth on exactly what happened during that time than the information that I'd been home schooled with.

The first contact occurred during the years I was in stasis. The Laldoralin finally decided to show themselves to the people of Earth, and who could blame them? Earth, or at least the human part of it, was quite frankly on a species-wide slow-moving death spiral, all of our own making.

Humankind had gotten to a point where all the societal niceties were breaking down, and fights were breaking out constantly, on both large and small scales.

The people in power had become so expert at manipulating the masses that much of humanity didn't know up from down, truth-wise. When you're in a state like that, you cling to your own viewpoint with a tenacity once reserved for preserving your life. Long-time friends and allies turned on each other, while other nations laughed in the background, not realizing that destabilizing the world for the enrichment of a few was a fool's gambit if our civilization was to survive.

I once read a novel by a great science fiction writer of the past that referenced the crazy years. The 21st century was our crazy century.

Krizon and his subordinates watched a sentient species, of which there are far fewer in the galaxy than planets that could be colonized or terraformed, slowly slip into madness. And from what I learned, we weren't the first species to have that happen.

The Laldoralin finally decided to step in when nuclear silo doors were being opened simply to intimidate, to rattle sabers. We were close to the brink.

I don't know if Krizon's having fathered human–Laldoralin offspring had anything to do with it, but he made the command decision. Save the humans from themselves.

They used the one thing that always worked with the human race. Shock and awe.

One day, half the Laldoralin fleet showed up over the cities of Earth. Huge spacecraft hovered over many of the largest population centers of our world, and yes, as expected, caused a panic. It was like every alien invasion fiction video that's been produced; the only thing missing was streams of laser fire disintegrating everything in sight. Instead, the "invaders" did something even scarier.

They hijacked everyone's personal entertainment/communication devices. Talk about an attention getter.

The only thing they did, was project on every device in the world, the words "Greetings. You are far from alone in the galaxy. Don't you think it's time to start acting like adults?"

Then they left.

The Laldoralin were not gone that long, maybe three months. It was just enough time for the shock to wear off and for humanity to realize that maybe it wasn't such a healthy idea to be constantly fighting amongst ourselves when there might be even larger issues to worry about. Those three months weren't pretty, but maybe the chaos was necessary.

When they returned, the "Dallies" did one thing that could be construed as an act of war. They neutralized Earth's nuclear weapons. All of them. All the nuclear materials in the warheads suddenly went inert. No more chemical weapons either. They took away the ability to quickly destroy ourselves in one fell swoop. Most people cheered. The underlying anxiety of when we would annihilate ourselves was gone and suddenly losing that constant fear was like an oasis in the hot desert.

Not everyone felt that way. The United States of America's military, suddenly deprived of one of their main budget sinks, convinced the president at that time that they needed to attack these audacious aliens with everything they had. Using the age-old playbook of "fear anything different" they also convinced large portions of the House and Senate too. They were given carte blanche.

A few days later, in a joint effort of Army, Navy, Air Force, and the fledgling Space Force, the USA tried very hard to go to war with a clearly much more advanced alien civilization. Russia tried also, but in both cases, the Laldoralin simply refused to cooperate.

The armed services used years' worth of munitions budget, literally hitting the alien flagship with everything they had in their arsenal. They might as well have been throwing snowballs. Having a pretty good idea how humans would react to their presence, the Laldoralin obligingly moved over sagebrush lands that were close to empty. Then, they simply raised all their shielding and as far as I know, settled down with a good book.

After several days of constant bombardment, a halt was called by the military, simply because they were running low on fireworks. A message came to them from their alien target: "There! Feel better?" It was kind of a smartass reply, and precipitated another forty-five minutes of attack, which had no effect whatsoever, other than to leave part of Utah a burned-out expanse of broken, burnt rock, and sagebrush embers.

"Let us know when you're ready to talk. We're ready now." Was the next message.

Even the hardest heads, in most cases, can understand when something just isn't working, so humankind dusted off an older, more retro strategy. One that hadn't been used much in many a year. They decided on diplomacy.

Ten years later, we had no more power problems, our environmental issues were starting to be solved, our recycling hit amazing numbers, and we had a legitimate plan for terraforming Mars. But none of those achievements were as amazing as the underlying one; we were starting to work together with each other again. We were starting to trust each other.

That may have been the most wonderful thing that our alien neighbors did for us.

Chapter Nineteen

"Here she comes," Dora's voice said quietly from Remora 2's side speaker. I glanced up and saw Lisa Beltran climbing down into the Probe Bay.

"How's the arm, Tanner?" Ensign Beltran asked. "First chance I've had to see how you're doing."

"A little sore," I said. "But the Kiffalan particle therapy seems to be doing the job."

There was a brief moment of distaste on her face, then it was gone.

"Really," I said. "It's not that bad."

"Excuse me if I don't want to test that out that alien tech first hand. It's good that your arm is getting better, though."

"Thanks."

"So, obviously, I heard. How's your mental state? Being stabbed with a flame knife… that's gruesome."

"I'm… okay. They're making us cadets out of stern stuff these days," I certainly didn't want to tell her that I was constantly looking over my shoulder. Or that I kept waking up fighting for my life as I emerged from nightmares.

"Maybe it has to do with that half Laldoralin DNA of yours?" she asked. "Maybe it makes you into 'stern stuff' also."

"Oh, so you know who I am, then?"

"The only thing that is faster than a jump drive," she laughed, "is the rumor mill on any starship. Though your eyes are so green they could only be… other-worldly. But, yeah. Some people are saying that's how you got onboard. I'm not saying that, though."

"There's a reason I'm on board, but that's not it."

"Y'know, I figured as much. Probably someone wanted to get you off Earth, and away from the E.F.E.," she said. "From what I heard, those guys tried to kill you on several occasions. Luckily, without success."

"You're well-informed, then. We had to move a lot. My foster dad had my sister and I trained in all sorts of survival things to try and give us a fighting chance. I can drive a getaway car, land or air, like you wouldn't believe. My dad, my sister, and I once trekked across the width of the Canadian Rocky Mountains with only a blanket, a knife, and a steel water bottle." I laughed. "Good times, good times."

"Sounds horrible."

"It was tough, but for that month and a half it took us, I didn't have to watch my back, I could just be. It was like having the world lifted off your shoulders." I hadn't contradicted her theory about escaping the E.F.E. I'd decided keeping my extra talents secret was a benefit to myself as well as the ship. Never let anyone see all your cards.

"That's good," Lisa said. "If I see anyone who even vaguely seems to have E.F.E. affiliations, I promise I'll bring the wrath of Kurakin down on their pointy heads."

"I am reassured, Ensign Beltran," I said, smiling.

"I have to go. P-7 was found in corridor 12-C beating his head against the wall. Literally. I've been assigned to review his behavior logs, and see where we went wrong. Someone probably gave him conflicting commands." She rolled her eyes, then got to her feet. "Have fun here in Remora land. And watch your back."

"Words of wisdom. Good luck with P-7."

She gave a mock salute and moved down the corridor out of sight.

"I think she may have been flirting with you, Tanner." Dora's voice came from Remora 2. "That comment about your eyes…"

"Well, they're almost aqua green, pretty unusual on Terra," I said.

"So it means nothing?"

"I dunno. It was complimentary, so I'll take it and be happy."

"She seemed to know a lot about you. Research?" Dora asked.

It gave me a moment's pause. "I think that what she said about rumors was true. Look how fast she came up with the sabotage angle when we first met. I kinda unburdened myself to my room-mate when I came on board, and evidently that info has been uploaded to the inter-ship gossip system. Whatcha gonna do?"

"It was unlikely to have been one of the officers. She didn't seem to know about your other abilities."

"Yeah. That's probably for the best," I said. "I think that is something we need to keep on the QT."

"Had I lips, I would zip them." Dora said. "Now, tell your mother how you are really doing. That was a terrible experience for anyone, but you are acting very dismissive of the whole thing."

"I'm fine, Mom."

"Please, Tanner. I'm not sure how you came to the conclusion that one of the most intelligent AIs in the neighborhood didn't have a clue, but I know you. You need to get this out."

I sighed, but she was right.

"I feel nervous all the time, Mom. Just this constant background stress that wasn't there before. Makes it hard to sleep."

I expected some sort of advice on how to feel good again, but Dora, for all her motherly ways, was a warrior.

"Then use it, my son. Don't let it get out of hand, but it is when you are most comfortable that you are most vulnerable. Use this stress to keep on your guard. The danger won't exist forever, but it exists now. Don't you forget it!"

"I read you five by five, Mom."

Chapter Twenty

The weeks went past, and we were nearing the first solar system. Commander Sharma had me at Alt-Tactical again.

The Remoras had miniature FTL drives and jump drives, and having very little mass comparative to the *Seeker* and no crew to be concerned with, R-1 and R-2 were sent ahead to feed our science section its first in-close look at this new system. R-3 and R-4 were sent on wide spirals on our lateral and vertical vectors, simply gathering data on this new (to us) area of space.

Lt. Vadslov was a busy man, unlike the rest of us in the secondary command center. He, and his counterpart on the main bridge, were processing data from the solar system as we approached. We knew something good was on deck when he whooped in triumph at his station.

"Yes! Planetary telemetry received, and it looks like out of the six planets we observed, we have a possible winner," he said.

"Talk to me, Gregor," Commander Sharma said.

"Second planet out appears to be only slightly smaller than Earth, and it appears to be blue. More data coming in… gravitational mass is .863 of Earth's. This is looking good," Vadslov replied. "Oh. This is interesting. Definitely a water world. Eighty percent covered with water."

"Land masses?"

"Some, but we still don't have enough info. Remoras are in mapping mode, Commander. We should have a holographic map within the hour."

"I wonder what the reaction is on the bridge," Ensign Ototototo said. "I mean, the main bridge."

"Yeah, we figured," Lt. Palmquist said. "They're probably as excited as Gregor is, particularly our Science Officer, Lieutenant Commander Torvald."

"So far, no signs of any technology or advanced civilizations," Vadslov said.

"If there's that much water, there might be an aquatic civilization, maybe down in the depths." Sharma replied.

"If so, then the Remora's scanning packages will detect it. The Laldoralins have charted more than a few aquatic species, and our scanning package has much of their tech in it. It's looking like an open world, though."

The Remoras were not only in communication with the *Seeker*, they were also communicating with each other. Each probe had a miniature jump drive of its own and if by some chance of fate something happened to us, all remaining Remoras would jump for home via a route of randomly calculated jumps to shake off any pursuit. No Remora would take the same path, greatly insuring that the data collected and news of our demise would be brought home. It would take a long while, as the probes were only capable of shorter jumps, but eventually, the truth would be known.

"Oh! Look at this," Gregor said. "Water planet has two moons, one of which has atmosphere, possibly oxygen! If we get a colony here, that could make for interesting dynamics."

We sat listening to Gregor's play-by-play, until we were relieved by fourth team. I knew that the main bridge crew was also rotating and wondered if Captain Yamashita would remain on station. None of us really wanted to be relieved, even though we weren't really doing much, but a new world was fast approaching, and everyone on board wanted to know as much about it as possible.

I decided to go down to the Remora bay and see if Truval needed any help. He was overseeing the guidance of the four probes, and I was sure he was monitoring the data feeds from each. Maybe I could learn more if I was helping. I had almost made it to the section when my Padd chimed.

"Cadet Tanner Voss, report to main bridge," a voice pronounced. I immediately turned and began retracing my steps, when I was brought up short. I hit the call back command on my device.

"This is Cadet Voss requesting clarification. Did you say 'main bridge'?"

"That's affirmative, cadet." The voice sounded irritated. "Captain wants you up here five minutes ago. Shake a leg, mister!"

"Aye-aye! On my way!" Some think it's undignified to run through a starship, but dignity never stopped me before.

The door to the Bridge cycled, and I entered into a space that seemed twice as frenetic as the Alt-Bridge. I walked near the captain's workstation and announced myself.

"Cadet Voss, reporting as ordered, Captain."

"Voss, good, report to Chief Kurakin at tactical. We may have a situation, I'll join you in a moment."

Kurakin was standing with a lieutenant commander I had only seen in the conference room, Commander Forbes.

"Commander," she said. "Voss is here."

"Voss," Forbes said. "Take a look at this. This is telemetry from Remora 3."

"It looks like…" I said, looking up from the screen he directed me to, "a ship. Is it any known species, sir?"

"It's not any design in our database, and our database is from the Laldoralin database," he said. "Which is not to say that our benefactors never keep things from us, but they were pretty adamant that they'd never come out this way. This one seems to be coming into the system from a fairly empty area of the region."

The image was quite detailed, even though Remora 3 was keeping a good distance away from our new arrival. The design was blocky, narrowing more to the bow and thickening toward the stern. Unlike the sleek hide of the Seeker, there were numerous protuberances, discs, trenches etc., which led me to believe that whoever had built the thing had done so in space. A closer look showed two modules, both with what looked like some sort of propulsion system.

"Is it modular?" I asked. "Those two lower sections look like they detach and become separate craft. Everything looks almost shabby, like it's very old and hasn't seen a space dock in a very long time."

"Impossible to say at this time," Kurakin said. "Science section is still analyzing, but my guess is yes. The lack of design aesthetics makes me think it's a warship of some kind."

"Do we think it's hostile?" I asked. I hated asking it but threat assessment was part of the tactical station's directed duties.

"That's why you're here, young fella," Forbes said. "Captain wants you to do that voodoo of yours and see if you can get a reading on them."

"Wow. They're a long way off, almost twelve billion, two-hundred-dred-forty million miles."

"How far away was the *Searcher* when you figured out the danger from the its destruction?" Kurakin said. "They were in Jump Transit, several light years distant."

"Point taken, Chief. Can I sit in this chair so I can concentrate?" Kurakin gave me a 'be my guest' gesture. Sitting, I closed my eyes and went inside myself. My 'danger sense' tends to activate strongly when I'm in immediate danger, but to get more subtle readings, I have to take the time to listen for it. I sat, listening to the voices around me, but also listening to something deep within.

I was feeling a vague unease, but not the sharp clenching I usually feel. "Commander, I feel… slightly unsettled, but that's it. Have they seen us yet?"

"I don't believe they have. It's entirely possible that they've got poorer scanning capabilities…" Forbes stopped when the captain stepped over to our station.

"Status report, Mr. Forbes."

"Our young Voss here feels… uneasy, Captain, but not immediately threatened. Do we want to send R-3 in for a closer look?"

"Can we do it without attracting their attention?" the captain asked.

"Honestly, I don't know," Forbes told her. "We don't have any idea of who we're dealing with. They might not even have Nth space communication ability. If that's the case, while we can see them in real time, anything they might be able to pick up from us would be hours old, maybe more. They do look like they've come from out-system, so there's a good chance they're either just passing through, or on the same mission we are."

"I may regret this, but have R3 go in for a closer look. Mr. Torvald," she said to the science officer, "see if we can learn a little more, without seeming threatening."

"So… fly R3 non-threateningly, then, Captain?" the science office asked.

"To the best of your ability, Mr. Torvald," she said, with a slight smile.

"Aye, Captain."

When you're called to the bridge, and suddenly you're put in a holding pattern, there's not much to do other than stay out of everyone's way. For me, this meant literally going to stand in the corner.

"Captain, telemetry from R1 And R2 coming in." Science Officer Torvald said. "The land masses have been mapped. Shall I display on holo?"

"Please do," Yamashita replied. "Ah… look at that. The land masses circle the planet in a loose ring, almost directly in what would be the planet's equator."

"Possibly formed by the system's solar gravitation in its early formation?" Torvald said. "Though much of this geology looks like igneous formation. Hopefully our new world isn't a burnin' ring of fire. If so, with all the vegetation we're reading, it must not be in a particularly volatile state at the moment. We'll be able to chart seismic conditions and history much better when we've had a few orbits up close and personal."

"Lieutenant, more telemetry from Remora 3 coming in," a female ensign, whom I assumed was under Torvald, reported. "From what I can make of this, the alien craft seems to have no biological signatures."

"Make sure you're not missing mineraloid or vegetoid life signs, Dark Feather," Torvald replied.

"Sir, there are no biosigns of any kind, or at least none that we recognize. I think it may be automated."

"Maybe run by AIs?"

"Maybe," Dark Feather said. "Could also simply be running by pre-set instruction."

"Or by remote control," the captain said. "Whoever it is, I'd prefer to stay friendly."

"So far, no indication that they've detected R3. No course changes, no change in any energy readings."

"All right, let's leave it at that; continue information gathering, and let me know if there is any change in status." The captain turned to me. "Tanner, you are dismissed for the moment. If you sense any… change in the danger level of our friends out there, report it immediately."

Chapter Twenty-One

I sat in the forward lounge, reading up on Shendra and Zuala's homeworld Kiffala, but I was having a hard time concentrating. We were coming up into what was likely going to be humankind's first non-system colony, and everyone was having a bit of concentration trouble. You could feel the excitement throughout the *Seeker*. It was slowly overcoming the paranoia.

I ran through name ideas, though the captain would decide on the actual name we'd call this new world. Oceanus? Pacifica? Atlantis? All names probably already considered. Maybe the captain would run a contest amongst the crew.

I wondered what it would be like to live on a world that was so aquatic. Sure, Earth's oceans took up two-thirds of its surface, but the land masses were still quite large. Not so on this new world. Barely an eighth of its surface was above water. Most likely, there would be no shortage of ocean views.

"Hey roomie, how's the arm?" Emil walked into the lounge, and seeing me, had come over and sat down.

"Getting better. These little Kiffalan repair motes really do the job."

"Glad to hear it. So, just taking some down time, then? Scuttlebutt has it you wound up on the bridge today. The real bridge."

"Yeah," I said, "we made contact with another vessel. Or, at least we scanned it. Hey, Emil? I need to ask you a kinda sensitive question. Did you tell anyone about my run-ins with the E.F.E? And by association, who I am?"

"I… um…" He looked embarrassed. "I might've let on that my new roomie was the famous hundred and sixty-year-old kid. I'm sorry Tanner, I was talking to a pretty girl, trying to make interesting conversation… I had no idea that someone would try to kill you. Or that we had an E.F.E. assassin on board. Dude, I am so sorry."

And there it was. You only have to tell one person in a closed community like this and it becomes ship-wide news.

"Can't be helped," I said. "But with a killer on board, we'll probably all need to be a bit discreet in information sharing."

"I hate this, man," he said. "Even if this slime-bag accomplishes nothing else, they've made it so that the entire crew is watching each other closely. With suspicion. This should be one of the greatest times in human history, and we're spending it worrying about knives in our backs and bombs in our beds."

"So. This new world," I said, trying to move back to more positive conversation, "you think the captain will hold a contest to name it? Maybe a lottery?"

Emil gave me a pitying look. "So young, so naïve. The naming of new worlds is purely her prerogative, and while I think the captain is pretty damn great, I have no doubt that ego, at least on this first world, will decide the name. Hell, she can call it Yamashita's World if she wants, and no one can say boo about it."

"Oooooh… she wouldn't do that… would she?"

"Probably not, it's not her style, but don't expect that name to come up for a vote. Make no mistake my young friend, she *will* name it."

Emil was right.

Though I had expected a little more originality from our CO, she did name the planet. I guess if she'd been Greek, it would've been named Poseidon, but since she was Japanese, the name of our new world was *Susanowo*, named after a Japanese kami deity of the sea. I foresaw difficulty for future generations, having to explain that there was no one named Susan involved.

Still, as names went, you probably wouldn't confuse it with that of any other world.

We smoothly slid into orbit around our find, and I can assure you, the forward observation lounges were in high demand. Everyone who wasn't on duty wanted to get a good look at this gorgeous new stellar marble.

I had managed to snag a spot on a couch near the main forward "port," a huge window that went up into the hull at an angle so that crew could literally have a floor to ceiling view of space, and just feasted my eyes on the planet. I was sitting between crewman Lana Canfield, a wide-eyed, freckled redhead, and crewman Lucius Carter, who had his curly hair groomed into a closely cropped sculptural pattern that was truly unique. We were all enjoying the views.

"Oh!" Lana said. "Look at that storm over to the left! It must be thousands of miles across! I wonder what it's like to be down in that?"

"Wet, to be sure. The way it's spinning, I'd guess that it has hella strong wind velocities," Lucius said. "Makes you wonder what colonists are gonna have to face when they set up down there."

"They'll have to be a hardy breed." I said.

"I dunno," Lana replied, dreamily looking out over the blue vastness, "I bet when the weather is good, it's like one long Hawaii."

"Or one long chain of the Aleutians." Lucius replied, grinning. I had a sneaking suspicion that these two trolled each other on a regular basis.

"No, the life ring of land masses lies along the equator. As does the orbit of the larger moon. Mr. Genova in planetary studies thinks that the two moons' gravity caused the volcanic activity that at one point caused these areas to rise above the water some time long ago."

"They say the larger moon also has atmosphere that could be gently terraformed into a suitable environment for colonists," I interjected.

"Really?" Lucius said, a skeptical look on his face. "I wouldn't want my kids to wind up like our Moonies, not even able to survive in one gravity without a ton of aid. They can't go anywhere except low-grav moons and planetoids."

I gestured toward the larger moon, just starting to show around the edge of the main planetary body. "Like, oh… I dunno… that one?"

"Hmmm." He looked thoughtful. "Point taken. It'd actually be a heck of a lot better place to live than our own moon, with a little terraforming."

In a mock secretive tone, Lana leaned my way and said, "He never concedes points that easily if I make them."

"You just need to make better points," Lucius said, a smile on his face.

Yep. If these two weren't an item, I'd eat my Padd. I mentally crossed Lana off my list of available partners.

My Padd chimed and Kurakin appeared on screen. "Cadet Voss, report to the bridge."

"Is there a problem Chief?"

"Possibly. The UFO has noticed Remora 3, and appears to be starting a pursuit course."

Chapter Twenty-Two

The bridge was abuzz when I reached it. Activity everywhere.

"Voss," Forbes called out to me. "Take tactical station three."

"Aye, Commander."

"Captain," Torvald said, "they are definitely in pursuit of our probe. Their speed just jumped twenty-five percent."

"Increase R3's speed. Stay out ahead of them. Torvald, prepare R3 for a micro-jump a few million miles out from where it is. Don't jump it anywhere near us. We don't want the bear to follow the dog home."

"Captain, enemy vessel has matched and exceeded R3's current speed." Torvald said, voice rising.

"Let's not call them 'enemy' just yet. Double the size of the jump you just programmed and get R3 out of harm's way."

"Aye, jumping now."

On the system map that holoprojected out of the H-deck in the center of the room, Remora 3's signal disappeared for approximately ten seconds, then reappeared far outside of the system, a long way from its pursuer.

"Alien craft is changing course," Torvald looked up from the screen. "Back to their original heading, Captain. They'll be out of this system in about two days."

Everyone visibly relaxed.

"Kurakin," the captain said, "I want you to go over the scans of that vessel and tell me everything about it that you can. I'm particularly interested in knowing how heavily armed it is. Just in case it decides to come back."

"Aye, Captain."

"And take young Tanner here with you. A junior tactical officer needs all the hands-on he can get."

The chief and I sat down at the secondary tactical station and began to pour over the data from R3. It soon became apparent that though the other craft looked a bit dilapidated, it was it was engineered for one task, crushing everything in its path.

"Wow," Kurakin said.

"Yeah," I replied. "Power readings are off the charts. And what is that opening at the front? A docking bay? A weapons array?"

"I'm guessing emitter of some kind. There's no indication of standard docking equipment, and there is definitely strong power generation in that area. And look at all these protrusions along the hull." She pointed to a series of boxy enclosures that radiated the length of the other vessel's hull. "Those look like old school missile pods. So many of them. And from what I can see, their scanning and information-gathering equipment is fairly limited. Quite frankly, I glad we can see them much farther away than they can see us."

"In full agreement here. I don't see any beam weapon pods, and R3 has scanned the exterior deep enough that they'd show up if recessed."

"This is a very odd setup. My guess is the missile pods are defensive. I'm also sure that these two major extensions are also ships, meant to operate independently." Her eyes narrowed. "I've studied battle strategies and tactical configurations of most of the Hegemony species as well as their enemies. None of them use this layout for ship-to-ship warfare."

"Not knowing what those supposed missile pods launch, it's hard to say what its ship-to-ship capabilities are. So many variables…" I had a rather awful thought. "What if its primary function is ship-to-planet warfare? If those are high yield missiles, depending upon the payload…"

"You could flatten cities, or worse. But we're speculating now. All we can definitively say is that this is not an explorer. With power readings like that, I'd assume they could have much better long-range scanning, but the ship doesn't seem to be built for that," Kurakin said. "Probably for the best that it just continues out-system."

"I do wonder though…" I said, "if it is fully automated or if we just can't get scans in deep enough."

"Not unless it's some completely new life form. R3 has a pretty amazing sensor package and there are no signs of any form of life we know or anything similar. Even if we're somehow wrong, and it's not a drone, it has enough weaponry and possibilities of weaponry that my recommendation to the captain will be keeping a low profile until that vessel is long gone."

I agreed with the chief in principle, but I was also aware that finding another species out here was a big deal. You don't just stumble across new races every day in the galaxy. Space is incredibly vast, planets are many, species that have made the climb to sentience, relatively few. Not that I had a vote in the matter. We would just provide analysis and the captain would make her decision.

As expected, she followed the chief's recommendation.

Susanowo proved to be a world a bit more volatile than our first scans had indicated. The *Seeker* began looking for an optimal location for a primary colony and found several that were stunning-looking. The land masses of the planet were in a string of islands circumnavigating the new world, most covered in rainforest; however many of the islands were volcanic. While most were dormant, there were some that could be problematic for colonists of the future.

The obvious solution would be to avoid those islands, even though they possessed some of the largest above-water areas. The problem was that those non-dormant volcanos could provide atmospheric problems down the line. The xeno-geology teams were working overtime to try and provide predictive models of what might happen, never an easy job.

When there is no threat on the horizon, a junior tactical officer is not much in demand. As I had no duties in that respect, I divided my time between the Remora Bay and studying my fourth-year subjects, jump drive engineering taking most of my study time, though it was starting to look like I'd never actually get near one.

I was studying in the forward observation lounge, when P-3 floated over to me. "Greetings, Cadet Voss," it said. "Chief Kurakin has new simulations that she wishes for you run."

"Battle sims?"

"Negative. The chief feels that you are sufficiently skilled in the area of tactical discipline. She has enlisted the aid of Lieutenants Truval and LeCosta, and Helmsman Kolara to provide alternative training for you. These simulations will all involve using the VR center. All will be EVA suit simulations."

I had a fair amount of Extra Vehicular Activity training at the Academy, but I found that the instructors there had nothing on the crew of the *Seeker* when it came to imagination. I was not in an actual suit, but the alien tech-enhanced Virtual Reality center was so convincing that you could've fooled a civilian with it.

My mentors had each helped program a scenario that would really put the screws to me. Truval and Kolara had given me tough ones, but LeCosta had sadistically given me a scenario almost impossible to complete.

Truval's was a fairly straightforward deep space Remora repair, based on traveling to the probe in a shuttle too small to act as a bay. Keeping myself and the Remora in place while I replaced the boards to the primary power plant was challenging, but not anything insurmountable.

Helmsman Kolara's sim almost took up where Truval's left off, except now I was on a small asteroid, and somehow my shuttle had become unmoored and drifted away. I was required to use the engineering EVA suit's arm panel to remotely pilot the shuttle back and land it on the small rock without crashing. This one took me three tries before I got it right. The simulated shuttle took more than a few unintentional detours before I got it down in one piece.

LeCosta's scenario was part video game, part manic revenge. In her test, I was not in an engineering EVA suit, but in one of the security force battle suits, roughly the equivalent of a two-legged tank. The first problem with this was that I had no experience in a Sec-suit, the second was that the test was a timed one, with me having to fight through several Klugg drones to the aft of the *Seeker* to restore power to the life support system. So far, the crew of our ship had died twelve times and I'd been shredded by the alien drones eight out of those twelve times.

To say I was frustrated was the understatement of the decade.

I was just getting ready to initiate run-through number thirteen when my Padd chimed and I froze the simulation.

"Voss? This is Chief Engineer Solas. Is Lt. Truval with you?"

"Er… no sir. I'm in the VR room doing sims from Chief Kurakin for my studies."

"Well, I need for you to get down to the Remora bay and find him. We can't raise him, or anyone down there, which tells me something's wrong with the comm system in that area. We're suddenly having some serious issues with the Remora transmitter we use to keep in contact with the probes."

"I'll head right down there, sir. If I can't find him, I'll come to Engineering. Maybe I can help with the probe transmitter."

"Thanks for the offer Cadet, but I have people, experienced people, on it. Thing is, they can't seem to find the problem. So, hustle down to the R-bay and find the master."

"I'm on it, sir."

"Hurry. Solas out."

Chapter Twenty-Three

I did hustle. People moved aside as I came barreling through, and a few sent sarcastic comments toward my backside as I passed, but Solas had sounded like this was an emergency. Ten minutes later, I was in the robotics division main area, and there was no one in sight.

This makes no sense! This bay should be crawling with staff.

"Hello? Where is everyone?" I said. "Anyone know where Lt. Truval is?"

Silence. Something wasn't right. We had Remoras outbound. The robotics bay was never this quiet when our babies were being deployed. Hell, it wasn't this quiet when they were docked.

I began to feel a clenching in my stomach.

Moving toward the Remora section, I stumbled over Crewman McNalley. She was out cold. Strong pulse, but totally non-responsive and it appeared she had a small burned area on the sleeve of her coverall. It looked like an electrical burn.

I moved over to the wall comm unit and tried to contact sick bay. The comm gave me the three standard beeps when a command wasn't accepted. I reached down to the Padd on my belt.

"Sick bay, medical emergency in robotics…" My Padd gave the same three failure beeps. How the heck did both the comm and the Padd go funky at the same time? I began to get a worse feeling. My stomach began its clenching cycle.

I moved farther in, and a short distance later found Chief Moreland face down on the deck, out cold and an electrical burn on his shoulder. His pulse was strong, but he wasn't waking any time soon. Looking up, I saw Truval laying on the deck in the Remora corridor entrance with his exo-skeleton all akimbo. He also was still alive, but I didn't know if his more rapid pulse was from injury or just his standard heart rate.

As much as I wanted to help the fallen immediately, it was time to go get security. I turned back toward the bay entrance, and saw one of the float bots at the control panel for the door control. The heavy pressure door closed and I distinctly heard the emergency lock engage. P-11, the bot in question, turned to me with interest.

"Subject Tanner Voss. High priority target. Switch to lethal ship defense tools," It said with a pleasant receptionist's voice.

I did not like the sound of that.

My body actually moved before I knew what it was doing, and a small melted area appeared on the bulkhead I'd been standing in front of. P-11 had fired its high-density beamer at me, the one for repelling possible alien attackers. The others had only been shocked, but evidently the person who'd tried to kill me earlier was in charge of the floater now.

"P-11, emergency shut down, authorization Voss-0617!" I said.

"Authorization denied."

"By whose authority?"

"Access denied." A red beam missed me only because I moved a half second before it fired.

There's a view port in every pressure door on the ship, it being a nice thing to know if the other side of a compartment entrance is open to space. I looked through the thick glass of the door the float-bot had just closed and saw Chief Kurakin and another security officer looking through it. I pointed furiously at the float-bot then spinning my finger near my temple to signify that it had gone crazy.

I guessed that Chief Engineer Solas, realizing that he couldn't reach anyone down here, had decided something was seriously wrong. None of that would help me, though. Getting the lockdown lifted, particularly if there were new passwords installed could take an hour or two. Cutting through the heavy bulkhead would take even longer.

I was on my own.

P-11 was trying to angle around to get a better shot at me, and I grabbed a data-spanner from Moreland's belt and winged it at my floating nemesis. It hit dead on, but the floatbots are made to do everything from outer hull work to assisting with ship defense. I barely scratched its paint.

"Cease all hostile activity," P-11 commanded, while sending a lethal beam at me, melting a small divot in the bulkhead that a moment before had been behind me.

"You first, P-11. You are firing on an authorized crewman of this vessel. Deactivate yourself!"

The bot seemed to stutter in its flight for just a moment, as if it was trying to fight whatever malicious programming it was running on, but it quickly recovered and took another shot at me.

"This is getting me nowhere," I muttered to myself. I turned into a side corridor that I knew looped back around back to the main bay, trying to get a little room to think. This was an engineering area, what could I use to deactivate or destroy a misbehaving murder machine? We had everything from plasma welders to antigravity lifters, but none of them were fast enough to do the job before I had numerous smoking holes in my person.

Looking ahead, down the corridor, I saw my answer.

"Oh, just keep looking in the wrong spot, P-11. Thirty seconds and I can level this playing field very nicely."

Floatbots are not meant to be hunter-killers. While P-11 did figure out where I'd fled to, it took his scanners a while to pick up enough genetic residue from my sweat to confirm that it had made the right choice in paths to murder me. When he finally caught on to where I'd scurried, I'd already had time to plan a defense.

Interesting fact about T.E.F. ships: the engineering department has access to two different types of E.V.A. "space" suits. The Mark Ones are the standard suit, designed for repairs in decompressed compartments, or light repairs on the exterior hull.

Then, there are the Mark Twos, and they are designed for tough times. The only suits more armored and shielded are the Security force battle suits. The engineering version is designed to be able to withstand everything from lightning bolts to gamma ray discharges. You could saunter around all day in a Mark Two on the sunny side of Mercury, and not even get a sunburn. They also multiply the occupant's strength by about a factor of ten.

When P-11 found me, it instantly flashed me with its beamer, which the Mark Two suit I had entered shrugged off like it was a hit from a squirt gun. As for myself, I didn't respond with the built-in right arm arc welder or the left arm plasma cutter. My response was much more direct. I punched the little mechanical bastard in the 'face.'

When it hit the far wall, P-11 looked like a fallen soufflé.

I made my way back to the main entrance, and depolarized my faceplate so that Kurakin could see it was me. I tried the suit radio to no avail. It was obvious we were being jammed, so I fired up the portable light screen from my wrist array. I set the font to large and typed in; "Being jammed, floatbot disabled. Will seek out jammer."

Kurakin held up her own Padd and pointed to the screen, "Someone has sent tight beam transmission at alien craft. Has changed course toward us. Find transmitter and disable!"

I gave her the thumbs up sign. This was why I'd originally come down here, trying to find Truval. I saw her speaking into the Padd. She held up the screen for me to read.

"You are likely not alone in there, be aware!"

I gave the OK sign this time, and hoped that the tech working on the door could get the damn thing open soon. In the suit, I might've been able to break out the door's large window, but that would leave part of the ship open to decompression if something catastrophic happened in here in the bot bay.

I searched each bay and corridor, trying to find any indication of problem hardware. I found two more unconscious crew persons, neither of whom I knew. I carefully moved each of them into the small alcoves that lined the corridors, knowing if anything happened in here and I was forced to use the suit for violence, I didn't want to step on any friendlies.

Since I had been attacked by a float-bot, I searched that side of the section first, but found nothing. I wasn't even sure what the heck I was looking for, and, assuming this was the same person who'd attacked me with the stealth suit, would I even be able to see it if I came across it?

Finally, I wound up in the bay for Remora 2 and 3, and was

rewarded with success. There, stuck into the Remora Comm socket for the absent probes, was a small notebook computer of some kind and it was hard-wired into the system through some old-style cables. It was encrypted, of course and my attempts to hack through my suit interface were a waste of time.

Did I dare just tear it out? Would it explode, or cause an explosion? As I stood there pondering, I felt that familiar clenching in my gut, and found myself dodging sideways. Unfortunately, the Mark Two suits are meant for ruggedness and strength, not agility.

I felt a huge impact to my port side and I spun like a top from the impact. I found myself looking at my own reflection in the polarized faceplate of another Mark Two suit. I barely got a block up for the next punch that came right at my own faceplate.

I didn't bother trying to communicate. Whoever was in there had made their intentions quite clear at our last encounter. The person who had attacked me had evidently had some fight training, and balancing a quarter ton of suit on one leg, gave a pretty passable kick at my midsection. Once again, I couldn't move fast enough to avoid it completely, and was rocked back on my heels.

Obviously, this was not a good time to fight defensively. Another punch came in, and I blocked it across my body. Stepping to their starboard side, I spun counter-clockwise and brought the suit's elbow up, coming around right into my enemy's face plate, the weakest point on a Mark Two. It didn't shatter, but it certainly cracked.

My opponent staggered backward, and I saw a large jagged split in the transparent titanium and a small section that had broken loose. Whoever was in there decided going toe to toe wasn't going to work, and I watched them access their arm holo-panel interface. A half second later, both their plasma cutter and arc welder began to glow. This was going to get really ugly.

"Why are you doing this?" They heard me, evidently suit-to-suit comms working, and looked up when I spoke. They chose not respond, but someone did.

As I stood there, firing up my own cutter and welder combo, a voice came over my helmet speaker.

"Tanner, are you alright?" At last someone had overridden the jammer!

"Yes, please identify."

"Why, this is your moth… this is Remora 2. I am just outside the pressure hatch behind you. Who is that you are conflicting with?"

"Unknown," I said, watching my opponent, "but they're challenging me to a plasma cutter duel, and they've over ridden all the controls in here. Can you override the override? Kurakin and her team are locked out of the bay."

"I'm sure I can. How can I help you though?"

"Can you close the interior blast door leading to this sub-bay?" I watched my opponent warily approach. The door behind them closed.

"Done."

"Great! Now, open the outer door to space and kill the gravity in here. Quickly please." I said, dodging a long shot of hot plasma.

"Your suit condition is green. Hang on!" As she said it, I used my helmet interface to mag lock my feet to the deck.

As my opponent charged in, the flashing lights of the opening bay door played across the cracked reflection in their faceplate. Even in my heavy suit, I could feel the force of the air rushing to space. And my opponent realized their predicament a moment too late. Blown off their feet, they sailed past me and slammed into the half-open door, desperately trying to get a hold on something. The door continued opening and, unable to get purchase on its surface, my opponent went sailing into space. Finally, comm silence was broken as a ragged scream came from my helmet unit.

"Oh dear, Tanner," my AI mom said. "I just did a voice scan on your assailant. It's… Ensign Beltran."

Chapter Twenty-Four

"What!?" I stood there, locked to the deck with helmet swiveled far enough to see the fading figure. I was in shock. This person who had befriended me, who I had been very interested in, was the person who had tried to kill me?

What do I do?

"She is losing oxygen from her suit at an astonishing rate." Dora's voice spoke quietly from my helmet speaker. "Are you going to save her?"

"I don't… I…"

"I am able to lock down her suit so she can't move, but my physical retrieval module is not currently installed, only my sensor package. If you wish to save her you will have to do it yourself. The choice is yours," Dora said. "However, she will be without oxygen in about seven minutes, give or take."

Could I save her? Did I want to save her?

Yes. If nothing else, I want to know why.

"Remora 2, can my suit jets match her velocity?"

"Not by my calculations; she hit space at an impressive velocity. However, I could ferry you to her easily." There was almost a nonchalant sniff in her tone. "If you want."

It was the same tone she'd used on me when I was ten years old, a century and a half ago, the one that said, "If you don't do the right thing, I *will* be disappointed." I didn't need prodding though. As angry as I was, I didn't want one of the first acts at this new world to be an execution.

"I am exiting the ship, if you could meet me. Also, can you do something about the transmitter? Kurakin said it's calling the alien vessel to us. I also need to talk to Kurakin and let her know what's happening."

"I will attempt to find the source and neutralize it." Dora said. "Time for a piggy back ride, Tanner. Wow, does that bring back memories."

I half grinned as I grabbed on to her hull and locked one of my gauntlets in a tow suspension point. We started forward gently, picking up speed as we vectored away from the *Seeker*, and in the distance, falling toward the planet, I saw Lisa Beltran's EVA suit. Behind her, *Susanowo* hung like an artist's canvas, rich blues and greens painted on a planetary scale.

"I have established a link with Chief Kurakin."

"Tanner? This is Kurakin, what is your status? Where are you?"

"I am E.V.A., ma'am. Hitching a ride with Remora 2 to retrieve my assailant who is in free fall and losing oxygen through a damaged suit." I couldn't help a slight hesitation, I still didn't want to believe the assassin was Lisa. "Chief, R-2's scans indicate that the saboteur is Ensign Beltran."

Silence.

"That is… unfortunate. Are you sure it's safe to bring her back on board? We have two heavy engineer's suits missing, and I assume one of them is her."

"With Remora 2's help, I have locked her out of her own system and frozen her suit's hydraulics. She's in a mobile brig cell now, but she's running out of oxygen."

"All right, bring her in if you can, but do NOT risk yourself. If something seems fishy, I expect you to let her go to her just reward. Clear?" Kurakin said. "The captain wants you back on the bridge as soon as you are in the airlock and pressurized. Evidently, Beltran was beaming transmissions at the alien robotics-ship, and now it knows we're here."

"What's it doing?"

"It's turned toward us, but Torvald is distracting it with Remora 3. Hopefully our probe can get it to chase the small fry out of the system then vector back to us. Get back here as soon as you've snagged her."

"Aye, Chief."

Matching speeds in a heavy-duty suit, in an environment with no oxygen friction to slow you down, isn't that easy. However, if you have one of the most advanced interstellar probes that your world can produce backing you up, the job becomes a lot easier.

Lisa was turning end over end in her trajectory toward the atmosphere, and I could see a faint stream of ice crystals coming from the smashed faceplate on her suit.

"Mom," I said, knowing we were on a private frequency, "is she locked down?"

"Affirmative. She can't do anything while she's in there," Dora said as I reached for one of the lift rails on Lisa's heavy EVA suit. "I can get us back to the *Seeker* fairly fast, but I have to adjust so that I don't damage the two of you with inertial gravitation."

I had a hold of the other suit now and I noted that the stream of crystalized oxygen coming out was getting thinner and thinner.

"How long do you think she has?" I asked.

"Her reserve tank has been engaged, but as her suit tries to save her, her atmosphere simply leaks out. Earth really needs to learn more about force field technology for emergency decompression situations. Do you have anything to make a temporary patch with?"

I wracked my brain for a solution. Each suit has various materials for spot repairs for the ship, though large damage effects are treated by support from central stores and repair bots.

I flicked open the supply chest that resided on my upper left arm, and rotated it so I could see the contents. The various small tools wouldn't do me much good, but I saw one thing that could do the job: Panel Goo. The viscous metallic compound was fired from a one-time-use gas-propelled tube, and was intended to spread out in a wide area to seal a smallish tear in the ship's hull. If I fired it full strength at Lisa's helmet, it might well take her head clean off, or at least destroy the neck seals on her suit.

I worked a small laser cutter out of the sleeve chest, working one-handed, and realized that I somehow needed to secure Lisa so I could use both hands. I solved the problem by putting her at my feet and magnetizing one of my boots to her suit's chest plate. Surfing with the enemy.

Remora 2 was coming around back to the ship in a wide parabola, intended to intercept the ship in its own trajectory without flattening me and the prisoner against the sides of our suits. As I carefully made a small hole in the propellant housing of the "goo shooter" to bleed off some of its force, I saw the we had swung around enough that the *Seeker* was almost between us and the planet. Our huge explorer ship looked like a tiny bathtub toy out here among the stars.

I had emptied enough of the propellant out of the Panel Goo tube that I was pretty sure I could fire it at Lisa's helmet without causing further damage. Magnetizing my other boot to her chest, I aimed it at her head and depressed the trigger.

The repair goo was indeed designed to spread out, but I had hoped to limit that somewhat with a lessened velocity. What I'd hoped for, and what happened varied quite a bit. The goo hit and spread, sealing the damage to her faceplate and covering most of the front of her Mark Two, including my feet. Did I mention that the sealant hardened almost immediately on contact?

The people who maintained the Mark Two engineering suits were not going to be happy with me.

Chapter Twenty-Five

"No, don't try to separate them, just clear the back seals so we can get them out of there."

A few minutes later, I was out of my Mark Two, sweatily standing in front of Chief Kurakin as they opened the other EVA suit. As the rear of that suit swiveled open, the two security people with the chief hauled out the occupant. Dora had been correct in her scans. It was Lisa.

"Ensign Beltran," Kurakin said, a cold tone to her voice. "You have some explaining to do. Smithson, take her to the brig."

"What the hell, Lisa? Why did you want to kill me?" I interrupted the chief's order, but I really wanted to know why this person who had befriended me had so enthusiastically tried to end my life.

"Earth For Earth, Tanner," Beltran replied, with a tiny hint of regret in her voice, though that could've just been my imagination. "Earth For Earth, not demons."

Of course, I had known in my mind that was the basic truth of things for her, but my heart hadn't wanted to hear it. I was her enemy, and she'd done what her superiors had ordered her to do regarding the 'alien menace.' Eradicate it.

I felt like the ground in Utah looked after the army had tied to bomb the Laldoralins. Bleak. Burnt.

"Save me from fanatics," Kurakin said. "Get her out of here."

As Crewman Smithson escorted our saboteur out of the Bot Bay, I noted that all the crew who had been laid out were gone, to sick bay I assumed. P-11 still lay in one of the corners.

"Chief? You'd probably better order all the float-bots into shutdown mode," I said. "Maybe even all the bots onboard, except the Remoras."

"Had Commander Solas do that with his override codes when I saw you dancing with P-11 in there. Right now, the *Seeker* is on manual mode. For the moment, though, you are needed on the bridge. Let's move."

When you are following behind a 6'2" Valkyrie who moves with the authority of Head of Security, you don't really have to worry about navigating crowded corridors. People naturally get out of the way if they see you coming, and a quiet "Make a lane" from the chief moved anyone not paying attention.

Everyone was on duty, even people who I knew were on other shifts. You never realize just how dependent you are on technology until it's suddenly shut down. Crewpersons were picking up all the duties normally done by robots; moving items on a-grav dollies, cleaning, minor repairs. It all had to be done, and a lot of it had been done by our resident AIs. The sooner the bots had their systems scrubbed, the sooner we could get back to regular routine.

"Reporting with Cadet Voss," Kurakin told the captain as we entered the bridge.

"You retrieved our saboteur, eh, Tanner?" Captain Yamashita said. "I'm not sure that her safety was worth risking yours, but we certainly do need to find out what other mischief she's been up to."

"Yes, Captain. I just… didn't want my first act over a new world to be an execution."

The captain nodded. "Well, she may have put us in enough hot water to boil the lot of us. Her broadcast to the alien vessel has alerted it to our position. We keep having Remora 3 lead it in another direction, but after a point, it always turns back to us, bigger game."

"That's not good," Kurakin said.

"No," Yamashita replied. "We're going to put the planet between us, then take a fairly large jump away from the system in the hope that we can get outside its scanning range and it'll lose interest. The last thing I want is to be the vanguard of a prelude to war with an unknown alien species. The only thing holding us up is that we're running another system diagnostic before we go to Nth space. No one wants a repeat of what happened to the *Searcher*. Ms. Beltran had access to critical systems in her duties as an engineer."

It was a chilling thought, but I had a feeling that Lisa had sent the tight beam to the alien vessel to get that craft to do her dirty work. Evidently, her own survival wasn't even a consideration.

"They've turned toward us again," Ensign Dark Feather announced.

"Mr. Torvald, status report on our diagnostic."

"We're eighty percent there, Captain," the science officer responded. "I suggest helm plots the jump from the other side of the planet and we start to move there. We'll be done with our system scan before we get to the jump-off point."

"Let's do it. Helm, you heard the man," Yamashita said. "Lay in an Nth space course from…. this location." She indicated a spot on the 3D map of *Susanowo*.

"Aye captain." Lt. Kolara replied. On the various view-screens, I could see we'd changed vector and speed.

"Captain," Commander Torvald said, looking up from his monitor, "Our friend out there is not taking Remora 3's bait anymore. Definitely heading our way now, in a series of micro-jumps."

"Here we go," Commander Forbes said, looking up from the primary tactical station.

"We'll not be starting an interstellar war," Captain Yamashita replied, "if I have any say in the matter. Time to jump point?"

"Seven minutes, ma'am."

"Captain, we've got a hang fire on the diagnostic," Torvald said. "There appears to be something wrong in the power regulation…"

"Helm!" the captain barked. "New directive, get us out of the planet's gravity well! All hands secure yourselves for possible emergency maneuvering." She repeated that command into her chair's intercom, broadcasting all through the ship.

I don't know if the captain had some sort of ESP premonition power, but her command was very well timed. Four minutes outside of the influence of Susanowo's gravitation, we lost main power.

I was not assigned a station, but I had managed to keep one hand on the railing around the main bridge. When main power died, the gravitation plates went with it, and I felt my feet start to drift from the deck. Using the rail for support, I forced my feet down, and the mag strip, standard issue in every service shoe, gripped the metal deck. The emergency lighting, operating under its own batteries, came on and lit the strips of floor and ceiling e-lights.

"Everyone switch to hand comms," Torvald said. "Captain, I was monitoring the diagnostics, and I saw right where we were in the system when the sabotage packet activated. Lt. Bittt-Nurr in the computer system can probably isolate that problem area in minutes if she knows where to look. I was recording the process on my Padd, like I've have been doing since the first sabotage event. If the lieutenant has this info…"

The captain looked around the bridge for a moment, and her eyes landed on me. "Voss, Not much use for you here at the moment. Take that Padd down to the computer core and give it to Bittt-Nurr."

"Ensign Dark Feather, you were monitoring also," Torvald said, "so go with Voss and make sure the computer team knows exactly where to look. Both of you be careful. The ship has a lot of fail safes, but there will probably be unsecured gear floating about. Move it, double-time!"

"Aye, Commander. Let's go, Tanner."

I won't say that it was chaos on the trip to Systems Engineering, but when you take away something as basic as gravity, things are gonna get wild. Even though everyone had mag strips in their shoes, and the captain had given a few minutes warning, not everyone had been fast enough to get secured to something.

As Ensign Dark Feather and I traversed the corridors, I saw someone in the dim light floating above the deck and gyrating, trying to reach a handhold. As we grew closer, I was slightly amused to realize it was Lt. LeCosta, my usually absent "handler."

There was no running in this environment, so by the time we'd reached her, she had rotated to a head down position. As we passed, I quietly reached out, grabbed her open thigh pocket and gently pulled her feet toward the floor.

"Er… thanks, Cadet," she said, face slightly red.

"No worries, LT! We'll get this sorted shortly!" I called back over my shoulder.

"Heads up," Dark Feather said, saving me from running forehead first into a floating socket driver that seemed to have my name on it. I ducked under, grabbing the tool and clipped it to my belt.

In general, on a vessel with a potential for a weightless environment, you wouldn't have loose gear that could take off on its own if the gravity plates failed, but where there are horizontal surfaces, objects will collect. During our adventure, I dodged various tools, a loose Padd, a runaway shoe, and a very aggressive coffee cup.

We reached the computer core and I saw Lt. Bittt-Nurr clinging to the side of the core by the tiny spurs that sprouted from each of her eight legs. She was holding a notebook computer that was linked into the core, and I could see the core was still powered, having its own energy source, independent of main power. One thing the E.F.E. hadn't been able to bypass.

"Ah, young crew," she said through a vocoder, "have you the needed log? I may have to reload the entire operating system from backup, minus the packet that has been introduced."

Dark Feather handed her the Padd. "Lieutenant, the captain wants you to know that we may have a hostile craft coming our way. Haste is in order."

"Yes, that is a reasonable conclusion," Bittt-Nurr said, her multiple eyes scanning the data. "You have delivered the needed information, please remove selves to areas outside of working zone."

That was possibly the politest way I've ever been told to get out of the way. Dark Feather and I moved to the side of the room, near the door as our arachnid colleague began working. She moved with speed that no human could match, assisted by two human ensigns I'd not met. Working on the core while watching the Padd she carried, I couldn't read the lieutenant's emotions, having little experience with sentients from her world, but I soon saw one of the ensigns begin to grin, and a moment later, the other one yelled "Yes!"

Bittt-Nurr came toward us, the lack of gravity seeming to have no effect on her at all, and handed Dark Feather the Padd. "Main power will be restored momentarily. Return to captain, and inform her please. Expect gradual return of gravitation."

"Aye-aye," I said.

Dark Feather and I began to retrace our route, and I could feel my body gradually getting heavier. After a short while, I heard a quiet click from my boots indicating that the mag strips in them had deactivated.

"You think that alien probe is still coming toward us?" I asked my companion.

"Their scanners didn't seem to be as good as ours, so hopefully, when we literally went dark, they may have lost us." Dark Feather said. "If not, we're going to be in trouble, because most of our major systems don't restart at the drop of a hat. Power feeds prioritize scanners, engines, life support and then everything else."

"Let's hope you're right. We have no idea what they have weapon-wise, and I'd hate to have to find out while our defensive systems are off-line."

The main lighting came on as we moved toward the upper bridge deck. It was a good sign, overall, lighting was fairly far down the priority chain.

Dark Feather and I entered the main bridge and the captain merely glanced at us and nodded. She returned to the science section and I sat in the third seat at tactical. Much to my dismay, the weapons board was still dark.

"Chief, why don't we have any weapons yet?"

"Our Ms. Beltran's little surprise has compromised our restart. We're having to re-power each system one at a time, in sequence. Weapons are sixth on the list."

"Behind?"

"Behind scanners, engines, defense fields, thrusters, life support. The captain wants to see what's coming and be able to maneuver before anything else. I would have prioritized weapons before life support." Kurakin shook her head, her short blond hair falling over one eye. "We're a little cold, and the air's a little stuffy... but, I'm not in command."

I hoped the captain wasn't making a big mistake, but as the chief said, not in command.

"We have F.T.L. control, Captain," Lt. Kolara said from the helm.

"Scanners are coming online," Commander Torvald chimed in.

"Status of enemy vessel," Captain Yamashita said, definite stress in her voice.

"They are... oh.... my... Enemy vessel is one hundred fifty-seven thousand kilometers away."

"How the hell did they... never mind. Helm, do we have thrusters yet?"

"Just went green on my board, Captain."

"Get us moving away from them. Best possible speed."

"Aye, ma'am. Best we can do right now is half light speed."

It was meant to be said to herself I'm sure, but Yamashita muttered under her breath, "I swear, if we get out of this, I'm going to space that little bitch." I was glad I wasn't Beltran at that moment.

"Captain," Ensign Dark Feather said, turning from her board, "the enemy vessel is separating into three modules. The two smaller pods are spreading out away from their mother module, and I read energy buildups in what we theorized are their weapon pods."

"Status of defense fields?"

"Sixty-five percent and rising, Captain," Kurakin said.

"Captain, I recommend prioritizing weapons over life support," Commander Forbes said from the chief tactical officer's station.

Yes!

"Lt. Grizik," Captain Yamashita turned toward the engineering station, "weapons next in start sequence."

"Aye, Captain," Grizik, a rather hairy humanoid from Galas-Pa, replied.

I had a complete set of weapons controls at third tactical, as did Kurakin at second. I watched my board for signs of life and saw Forbes' board begin to flicker. He had control of the big particle cannons, while Kurakin had the missile system. I was in charge of point defense beamers and the asteroid gun, which was actually used for mining.

Any station in our section could take on all three duties at once, with Forbes station being able to override either of the two junior stations if he felt it was necessary.

I saw Kurakin's board light up, and a few seconds later, my own had power. Weapon systems were green. Forbes told the captain as much.

"Lt. Tarpin," I heard the captain say, "Attempt to broadcast to them that we are on a peaceful mission. It may be an automated probe, or it may be controlled by an AI that we can have a discussion with. Either way, we need to try to avoid this battle if we can."

"I don't think we're going to be given that option, Captain," Commander Forbes said, without looking up from his tactical display.

"We have to try, Commander. I'll let you know when diplomacy fails. But, let's sound general quarters and get everyone to battle stations."

"Aye, Captain."

"Captain," Torvald called out from science station one, "the main module's got an energy spike from that front array. Power levels are extremely high."

Then I got that feeling, and it was as bad as when the *Searcher* almost creamed us. I had to say something.

"Captain, we must go hard to port, now!" I said it with vehemence, and I could see her look at me in surprise, mind going over the fact that a cadet had just dictated to her on her own bridge. It took her three seconds to work around to my earlier performance that had saved the ship from destruction, five seconds that seemed like forever to the terrible tension in my gut.

"Helm! Hard to port! All starboard thrusters fire now!" She said.

Without that three second delay, I'm pretty sure the enemy would have missed us.

Chapter Twenty-Six

I was still shaking my head a minute later, trying to clear the fog.

What happened? Then I remembered, we had taken a terrible hit. Bridge lighting was just coming back on, and I saw the captain climb back into her command chair. There was blood trickling down her forehead. Kurakin and I had both been strapped in, as was most of the bridge crew. Notable exceptions were commanders M'Buku and Forbes. Both had been thrown across the deck, and now lay unmoving in a corner. I could feel that we were tumbling, as everything not nailed down was drifting toward the outer edges of the room.

"Status report! Stations sound off!" The captain yelled.

"Main drive still online," Lt. Kolara said. "I've lost power to starboard thruster packs in the forward section though."

"Get us on an evasive course, best possible speed."

"Defense systems are still online," Kurakin told her, "all those except point defense in in the forward starboard section."

"That's where we were hit then. Prepare all weapons to fire back. I'd tell Commander Forbes that diplomacy has failed, but I don't think he can hear me," the captain said. We all looked where a medic was examining Forbes who still lay unconscious.

"Tanner, I'm going to take over point defense," Chief Kurakin told me. "I want you to take the main particle cannons. Punch back hard, Cadet."

Oh, damn, this got real very fast. I took a deep breath.

"Aye, Chief." My board indicated that the main guns were now hot at my station. Time to put up or shut up.

The ship was spinning and tumbling still, but the helmsman was getting us under control, and flying one direction. It was evident that we'd taken an oblique hit.

"Damage report!" the captain said.

"Captain," the damage control officer said, an incredulous look on her face, "The starboard bow, section One-B... is gone."

Her seat was next to mine, and a three-dimensional display of the ship shown on her overhead monitor. A small neat crescent section of the nose of the ship was gone, cut away without so much as a jagged edge. Simply obliterated. The board read that the area had been automatically sealed off, but I wondered how many crew were there when we were hit.

"Return fire. Fire at will."

Following the captain's order, I let my targeting computer orient the main cannons toward the main enemy module, then switched over to manual. Eyes half closed, I felt for the target in my mind. When the tension felt just right, I pressed the firing control.

I hit the target dead on, for all the good it did.

"Direct hit, captain," Torvald said from Science. "Beam hit a field and then was curved away from the target. Some sort of magnetization field like our own deflection fields, only a lot more able to deal with beam weapons."

"The module closest to us, designation Beta, is launching what looks like a missile swarm," Ensign Dark Feather said.

"Tanner, switch to point defense system," Kurakin said, a grim look on her face. "Take out as many as you can before they get to us. I don't want to have our own shielding overwhelmed."

"Aye-aye, switching to point defense." I reconfigured my board for the smaller stutter-fire beam weapons. As I switched over, the third module, designated Charlie, also fired a barrage of missiles. The strategy was a strong one: overwhelm another vessel's defenses with alternating missile swarms, then fire that massive beam weapon to vaporize as much of your enemy as possible.

Not on my watch, jerkbags.

As the first swarm got close enough that we no longer needed Nth space scanning from Remora 3, I manually aimed the defense grid. The computer chimed, warning me that the enemy missiles were still out of range, but computers and I had often had disagreements on that sort of thing before. I usually won.

"Missiles seem to be pure energy," Dark Feather announced. "Like the Thunderbird's bolts."

"Tanner, can you do this manually? They're moving very fast," Kurakin said.

"Give me a moment," I replied. "Here we go."

I began to fire the point defense beamers in sections, rather than the normal practice of just cutting loose with everything on the board. There was a method to my madness, and I sunk down deep in my mind and felt the incoming storm of destruction. My fingers danced over the console, seemingly with a mind of their own and I began to feel like a cross between a concert pianist and Shiva, Destroyer of Worlds.

The first salvo came in hot, and began exploding as my counter measures connected. It was helpful that the explosive yields of each was enough that they helped set each other off.

"Retract the bridge into the hull," the captain said to Grizik at engineering. "Let's not get chopped off at the neck. Actually, retract all extensions except long-range scanners."

The two smaller modules kept up a constant barrage, their energy missiles evidently highly replenishable. Each kept sending a barrage, staggered to roughly five-minute intervals on an alternating basis. I was able to fend them off completely for over an hour, but I began to learn my limits. And the limits of the *Seeker's* weapon systems.

I was sweating, having been concentrating hard since I took over the point defenses, and could feel myself tiring. To make matters worse, I could see some of our close defense emplacements were starting to redline and overheat. Add to that, the point defenses were getting low on power, and everyone could see that our strategy wouldn't work much longer. They needed to recharge, I needed a break, and the few missiles that were now getting through were draining our shields.

"Chief? Any luck on hitting that main ship with the mains?" The captain asked.

"Negative, the targeting computer is managing to hit it obliquely, but the beams then just bend away into space. Their own shield is a little weaker, but our inability to make a strong direct hit makes the power loss minimal."

"But there is a power loss?" I asked.

"Definite drop when they deflect our particle beams," Commander Torvald said from the main science station, "But I'm detecting a power build-up in that center section, to what I believe is the weapon they hit us with earlier."

"Tanner," the captain said. "If you feel anything, and need us to move one way or the other, tell Kolara at the helm. Don't even worry about stepping on my toes, just don't let them hit us with that thing again."

"Aye, ma'am," I replied as I detonated another missile barrage. This time three got through, and the Seeker rocked at the impacts on our own shield system.

"Captain," Engineer Solas voice came from the captain's intercom, "that last blast has knocked the jump fin array out of alignment, badly. We don't dare try a jump."

"Great, what else can go… no, let's not ask that question," the captain said. "Helm, are we staying ahead of them?"

"We're gradually pulling away, at sublight speed," Kolara said, "but, Captain, when we get a sufficient distance away from them, they'll be able to stutter jump right back on our tails. They don't seem to be interested in giving up, either."

"Captain, request permission to take control of the main cannons for a moment," I said. We'd been firing at the main module, fearing that another beam weapon attack was coming and hoping that since we were dealing with AIs of some sort, taking out the main module might take out their controller. "I wonder if those missile modules are as well shielded as the mother ship?"

"I am certainly willing to find out," Captain Yamashita said. "Chief, take point defense. Mr. Voss, do your thing."

"Aye-aye, ma'am. Chief? Can you give me control of our missile system as well?"

"You have mains and missiles, Tanner," Kurakin said.

I had an idea. I'm not sure where it came from, but the obvious problem we were having was the enemy's shielding. Rather than trying to nail a direct hit, I analyzed where the weakest point in those defense fields might be.

The nearest missile module was coming in for another launching of its energy barrage, and I had the targeting computer put me in the general ballpark of where its vector would take it, then I took over. I manually aimed the main particle weapons at that ship.

"Tanner, don't you want to hit them with missiles first? To soften their defenses?" Kurakin asked.

"I want to try something new…" I fired the main cannons and as they made contact, I fired every missile that we had loaded at the same spot that the beams had just hit. While they were on their way, I dropped the railgun into firing position and began its charging sequence.

"You're not going to try and hit a moving target with the asteroid cannon, are you?" Commander Torvald said.

"Trying something new," I said, waiting for the railgun to show green on my board.

"Missiles are impacting," Ensign Dark Feather said, looking up from her board. "They hit the same point as the particle cannon, captain. Shield strength at that point on the enemy module has dropped to twenty percent of previous."

I heard a grim satisfaction in the captain's voice. "Get them, Cadet. Hit 'em hard."

"Yes, ma'am." I said. The railgun went green, just as the main cannons showed complete recharge. I fired, main beam cannons, then the asteroid cannon. The beams hit the weakened shields, and traveling faster than the projectile, they caused no physical damage but dropped the module's shield strength even more.

When the railgun round, a composite of several heavy metals moving at thousands of kilometers per second, hit the enemy module it had hardly any shields left. The result was spectacular, in a velocity plus mass equaling energy kinda way.

The front half of the aggressor vessel vaporized, and the back half went spinning off into the depths of the galaxy, its forward momentum redirected by the blast. Debris was scattering in an expanding sphere in every direction.

The odds had just moved more in our favor, or so we thought.

Chapter Twenty-Seven

"So, have they given up?" the captain asked.

"I would call it regrouping, Captain," Kurakin replied.

We were once again in the conference room just below the bridge, while the secondary bridge crew filled in. There were high energy snacks and drinks laid out before us. We were allowed this break, because the remaining two enemy vessels had dropped back well out of range of our primary beam weapons.

We had been slowly, very slowly pulling away from our pursuers, and Commander Torvald had assured the captain that the science section would be able detect when the main module was attempting to hit us with the weapon that had clipped off part of our nose.

"They haven't given up pursuit," Commander M'Buku said. The XO had returned, his right arm held in place with a bio-sling. "But it's hard to know exactly where this is going to go, especially since we're not only working against what appears to be an AI, but an alien AI that we have no frame of behavioral reference for."

"I am beyond trying to understand motivations at this point," Captain Yamashita said. "They've given a very good account of themselves when it comes to their intention to destroy this ship and us along with it. At this point, I want to either know how to lose or destroy those drones."

"Commander Forbes is still in med-bay," Kurakin told her. "The tactical staff and I need time to formulate a plan of attack, or a trap that we can ensnare these things with. Also, we've been trying to get ahead of them for seven hours, and you'll notice Cadet Voss looks somewhat worse for wear."

"How are you doing, Tanner?" the captain asked.

"I'm a bit tired, ma'am, this is the first time I've had to use my... strengths for such an extended period. Just need a little cat nap, and I'll be right as rain."

The truth was, I had the mother of all headaches. Twice, I had felt that terrible feeling and yelled for a course correction. The captain's earlier order to the helm allowed an almost instantaneous veering off on our course, and both times we'd barely missed being nailed by a particle beam so powerful that science station said a direct hit would've destroyed the *Seeker* in one shot.

I just hoped that Torvald and Dark Feather could deliver on their promise of being able to detect when that weapon was about to fire.

"Solas," the captain said, turning to the chief engineer, "I've seen the readouts, but I'd like to hear your take on how badly we were hit."

"If we hadn't zigged when we did, ma'am, I think that shot would've quite literally vaporized the entire forward section of the ship. As it is, a corner of both observation lounges was chopped off, and part of the Exo-Botany lab. We have sealed off both areas, and are working on both hull repair and system bypasses. We've taken damage through misalignment of the jump fins, so we are currently unable to use the jump drive, unless we want to transit somewhere completely unknown or possibly wind up like the *Searcher*. We have minor damage to the FTL reactor, but can still maintain eighty-five percent thrust. Starboard forward point defense battery is still offline, but we're rerouting power feeds. Should have that back within the hour."

The captain rubbed the bridge of her nose, as if she too had the mother of all headaches. "How many crew? How many of my people were lost?"

"Almost all the crew were at their stations or their backup positions," Kurakin told her, "so very few people were in the affected area, thank God. However, Crewmen Davila and Smythe were in the officer's lounge area retrieving one of our wayward floatbots to take back to robotics. Both are missing, as is Dr. Petersen, who was in the botany lab."

"Why the hell wasn't she in the safe core? I believe I made it clear that we were at general quarters. Procedure is that all non-essential crew are to move to emergency stations."

"I don't know why she didn't heed the warning," Kurakin said, her hand spread out in a show of frustration. "I'm guessing that our onboard scientists need a refresher on what's more important than whichever experiment they happen to be running at that moment."

"When we get out of this, Chief, I will want you to remind them, in no uncertain terms, of procedures designed to keep them alive. Make it dramatic."

"Count on it, ma'am."

The captain dismissed me, and placed me under orders to go get some sleep. The only problem with that is when ordered to get sleep, often my brain won't cooperate. I did manage a twenty-minute catnap, which took my headache down to the background noise level.

I got out of my bunk, and took a quick shower, the recyclers catching every stray drop of water. After I felt clean, I stood there an extra minute or two and was dry by the time I stepped out. I also knew what I had to do.

The brig, the *Seeker's* version of jail, was at the bottom of the safe core, and it took a bit of determination to find. The closer I got to the heavier-than-normal hatch, the more I began to think this wasn't one of my more brilliant ideas, but what had happened felt like it was eating me from inside. I had to know why.

There was one security officer sitting at a small desk with a computer. As I entered, he looked at me in a very cool manner, not really wanting any complications in his day. No one was pleased that one of our security team personnel now had to be allotted to be a corrections officer.

"Would it be possible for me to talk to her?" I asked.

"Shouldn't you be conducting your duties, Cadet?"

"The bridge personnel are on a break, and the ship's being run from the E-Bridge," I told him. "The captain told me to get some rest, but I can't seem to get to sleep. I just… I just want to know why she wanted to kill me." I knew I was sounding whiney, but I didn't care. "She tried so hard to be my friend."

He looked at me with sadness in his eyes. "She tried to kill us all, kiddo. That should tell you who she really is. She's about as trustworthy as a scorpion, asking you to carry it across the river, promising she won't sting."

He had a point. Lisa had tried to kill me with a fiery knife, a robot, a plasma cutter, and a giant alien drone. The verdict on her success with the last one was still out. But I still needed to ask her, face to face.

"Could I still have a moment to talk to her?"

"Okay, but I will be monitoring and recording. And listen to me, I want no violence against that prisoner," he said. Since she was behind a foot-thick clear titanium cell door, I doubted that was even an option, and I was just there to talk.

He let me into the inner cell area. Lisa was in the enclosure on the far right, one of three cells, and it was pretty spartan: bed, sink, and a screened toilet area.

I palmed the speaker control. "Hello, Lisa."

She slowly turned toward me; resignation and hopelessness gave her eyes a flat, almost dead look.

"Why did you save me, Tanner. So you could come in and gloat now?"

"No! That's not it at all! You had some time to get to know me, Lisa. I'm not a gloater. I'm here to ask you one simple thing: why?"

She looked away from me, stared at the wall for a good ten-count, then turned back.

"You seem like such a nice guy, Tanner, but that's how your kind traps people. Traps their souls."

Was not expecting that.

"How the heck would I trap anyone's soul, Lisa? That's flat-out crazy talk."

"All those who have welcomed the invaders of Earth have jeopardized their souls," she said, looking at her feet. "The aliens are the Fallen Ones, come to corrupt as many as they can before the end times."

I was flabbergasted. I knew that the E.F.E. was fanatical, but was this always part of their weirdness? I hadn't had an inkling of this bit.

"Lisa, seriously? You know, every major religion on Earth has managed to make peace with the fact that Earth and its people are not alone in the cosmos, Lisa." I said. "Buddhists, Christians, Muslims, Hindus and almost all the rest. I find it hard to believe that anyone could still put so much faith into such a harsh and jaundiced view of other sentients."

"Those false religions will not save them in the end," she said. "From the time I was a little girl, I have been taught that I had a mission to save all the people on our world by helping to drive off the Fallen, to make them leave us in peace. To not let them destroy our souls."

"I just find it hard to believe that you actually believe I am some sort of demon," I replied. "That is majorly screwed up. You acted like you wanted to be friends, like you liked me, and I find out that it was all a carefully thought out strategy. You tried to kill me. You tried to kill everyone on this vessel. How the hell is that supposed to save anyone's soul, much less yours?"

Her voice was almost a sing-song as she replied. "I am a warrior for the people of the Earth, Tanner. If you are not a demon, then you are a demon spawn. If all the people of this ship, including my-self, are sacrificed, then the people of Earth will rethink this foolish venture and possibly force the Fallen to leave us in peace. If so, then the sacrifice is more than worth it."

We just sat there, both of us looking at each other. The security guard had been right. Trying to change the mind of a fanatic, espe-cially one trained from childhood to be a "warrior for the Earth," was a fool's errand.

I was not a human being, a fellow sentient trying to make his way in a seemingly cold vast galaxy, I was just a monster trying to cor-rupt... everyone. Any kindness I might give would just be a seduc-tion. I stood up from the short bench I was sitting on.

"I wish I could show you the truth, Lisa, but I know you would never accept it. There is simply no way to get through to you. Goodbye."

She looked sad for a moment. "Goodbye, Tanner. May all our deaths be swift and painless."

❖

I was able to sleep a little more after having wasted my time with Lisa. If nothing else, maybe security would have a little more insight into her thought processes. Her insane thought processes.

To say that I was unsettled by my talk with her was a huge understatement. For all her murderous intent, she was an intelligent person, but from what I had gathered, she'd been indoctrinated from a young age and the E.F.E. had been training her to infiltrate the Exploratory Force most of her life.

Crap like this made me sad. Not for myself, not just for Lisa, but for the human race. We were (and yes, contrary to what Lisa and her handlers thought, I considered myself part of the human race) a great contradiction. We've always looked at the stars and wondered. It has always been a war against what has been, and what might be. Some of us never want to venture out of our caves, and there is a certain survival wisdom in that.

Often, the adventurous were the ones the saber tooth ate.

But the ones who always wanted things to be the same, stay the same, were not the ones who figured out how to make fire first. The safe-in-the-old-ways-people didn't develop the bow, electric light, the jet engine, the lunar lander.

There are those on Earth who want to do things as they were done in the 19th century, and they don't bother anyone. They want to live the way they want to live, and they don't get in conflicts with other people. More power to them.

But even in this enlightened age that I once considered the future, not all are content just to do their own thing. There has always been a contingent so afraid of change, that they will do anything to stop the human race from going in new directions that they feel are unfamiliar.

You see it in every nation. It was almost like a mathematical formula: new equals different, different equals scary, scary equals bad, therefore new equals bad. New must be destroyed.

The Earth For Earth people would happily kill everyone on the three Explorer ships just to make everyone afraid of new frontiers.

It became too much for my tired brain to deal with, and I fell asleep again.

Chapter Twenty-Eight

"Cadet Voss, return to the main bridge, immediately." The speaker at the intercom and the one in my Padd spoke simultaneously.

I swiveled my feet to the floor, and realized my headache was gone. Using a wake-up towelette on my face, I left my room and hurried to the lift. I checked in with my gut and felt the tensing, but it wasn't too urgent, yet.

Things didn't look panicky when I hit the bridge, but everyone was definitely tense. I guessed our drone friends were up to something. The captain noted my entrance.

"Mr. Voss, the enemy is splitting up, with the remaining small module beginning to take another vector, though one still in our general direction."

That sounded suspicious. "Do we have any idea why, ma'am?"

"Commander Forbes?"

Forbes looked up from his display. He had fading bruises on the left side of his face and a health regeneration band around his head.

"From our analysis, I believe they are going to try to surround us, by having the main module jump ahead, while the secondary module comes up from behind. We would have to veer from our course, which would divert us from our direct path away from them. That might give the secondary time to catch up, while the main takes pot shots at us with its big gun."

"Have you had any time to formulate a counter plan?" Yamashita asked.

"We think so, though it would require some very close timing, Captain. The main module is the more formidable, and could one-shot us out of existence. It also seems to have the better propulsion system." Forbes replied. "Like all our ships, even the Laldoralin vessels, there is an energy flare a few seconds before jumping a ship into Nth space, residue from breaching the barriers between the two spaces. This drone is no exception."

"And when it jumps?"

"When we see the energy spike, we reverse course as quickly as the ship can bleed off inertia, and charge back toward the smaller module. We've been able to exceed the standard speed of the main module for some time now, and we believe with the element of surprise and the overcoming of inertia, we can organize this so we only have to fight one ship at a time."

The captain considered the plan for a moment. "That much inertial compensation will be a big power drain. The *Seeker* wasn't really intended for such maneuvers."

"But she is capable of them, ma'am. Solas and I have gone over the consumptive needs of the whole thing, and by the time we reach the smaller ship, he believes our power levels will have climbed back to ninety-five percent," Forbes said. "Our weapon strength, with a little pull from non-essential systems should be full up."

"So, pardon the cliché, the best defense is a good offense."

"We believe so, Captain."

Forbes and the captain stood for a moment, our CO digesting the implications of the plan.

"All right," Captain Yamashita said. "Bring us back to full alert. Mr. Voss, I want you to take lead on the weapons systems, splitting the labor however you see fit. Mr. Forbes, I hope this won't step on your toes too badly, but we can credit young Tanner here with one victory already."

"I'm good with it," Forbes said. Then looked at me. "However, Cadet, keep in mind that as far as we can tell, our enemies are going to require us to be three for three. So... no pressure."

Yeah. No pressure.

We moved toward the outer edges of the system and we waited. Our pursuers kept falling farther and farther apart, though not in any way giving up their pursuit.

"Are they going to do something?" Ensign Dark Feather muttered, barely loud enough to be heard.

"Tend your station, Ensign," Commander M'Buku told her. "Believe me, when this heats up, we'll all be happy for the times they were sitting there behind us."

"Yes, Commander," she replied. "It's just that, I don't understand why they're hunting us. We're just exploring. That world we were orbiting had no trace of any kind of civilization so why do they want to destroy us? We weren't threatening them in any way!"

If M'Buku took exception to a junior officer speaking so freely, he didn't show it. When he spoke, his voice was almost fatherly.

"We have no idea how old that vessel is, Ensign. It could be remnant of some ancient conflict we know nothing about. It could be the standard greeting of some highly xenophobic race or, God forbid, maybe we've landed in the middle of someone else's war. In any case, all we can do is defend ourselves and try not to make too big a ripple in our wake."

"Stay focused," Captain Yamashita said from the command chair. "We can sort out the 'why fors' after we get through this in one piece."

"Aye, ma'am." Dark Feather said.

I sympathized with her. We had made no hostile moves since we'd come to this remote bit of the galaxy, and had defended ourselves only when we had no choice. But we were definitely in a "destroy or be destroyed" scenario now.

As far as I was concerned, the solution was going to be the former, not the latter.

"Captain," Dark Feather said, looking up from her monitor, "Getting pre-jump emanations from the enemy main module and… Captain, the other module is also producing jump readings!"

"So, they do both have jump drives," Yamashita said. "Helm, new course, take us north axis, thirty degrees. Once on that course, return to full FTL speed."

I started to feel the tensing in my stomach, "Captain, they're coming!"

"Ready weapons, Mister Voss."

"Weapons are green, ma'am."

"Course correction made, resuming current maximum drive," the helm station reported.

"They're jumping!" Dark Feather said.

A second later, the two red blips on my screen reappeared. The main module had overshot us by over one-hundred-fifty thousand kilometers while the secondary module popped back into normal space less than fifteen thousand behind our current course. Had the captain not ordered our course correction when she did, they would have jumped in almost on top of us, and had a nice pincer attack vector.

"Enemy vessels are coming about; their weapons are hot," Torvald said from the main science station.

"Mr. Voss," the captain said. "Fire at will."

"Aye-aye!"

Both enemy ships had come out of jump space facing away from where we had currently repositioned ourselves, indicating that their scanning ability was not as advanced as the sensor packages on our remoras. They were rapidly correcting this mistake, but I made the most of their error.

Concentrating fire on the smaller module, I hit it with both the main particle cannons. Its speed dropped dramatically, which led me to believe it was drawing power from its engines to beef up its defenses. I began to pepper it with our point defense grid beamers.

"Shouldn't you use missiles?" Forbes said, "Those smaller beamers weren't meant to be hitting out that far."

"Their defense grid is having trouble compensating for the continuous multiple hits," Torvald said from Science.

What Torvald didn't see was that I was purposely hitting in a circle, surrounding the point where I had previously hit their shields with the mains. My gut was telling me that the enemy craft's shielding intensified where ever it was taking a hit, drawing power from unaffected areas.

"Now, we'll use missiles," I said.

I launched all our aft tubes, directing the missiles remotely, and I could feel Commander Forbes watching me. He hadn't been conscious when I had pulled off the last Hail Mary move, and was likely wondering why the captain was giving me this much leeway at his station.

I watched my boards, and saw the main cannons go green again, fully recharged. Just as that happened, my custom missile spread impacted in very close to the same flower pattern spread that the defense lasers had hit.

I felt the moment. My fingers stabbed down on the main cannon's fire button. The result wasn't quite as spectacular as the first module's destruction, but the beams definitely pierced the enemy module's defense field. A bright flare appeared at the point of impact, and small explosions broke out on that area of the vessel.

"Enemy module beta is damaged and losing attitude control," Ensign Dark Feather said aloud. She looked up from her display. "Scanners read their defense field is at twelve percent of normal!"

"Tanner!" the captain said.

I was way ahead of her. All the aft missile tubes had auto-reloaded and I had sent a second salvo on it's way as the main cannons had impacted. They hit the depleted shielding and tore through it like it didn't exist. Multiple explosions detonated on the drone's hull, and it began tumbling away. Scanner showed it still had areas of power still functioning, but there was heavy damage. Module Beta was out of the fight.

But the main module was not. I started feeling my gut go wild when Commander Torvald yelled, "Drone Alpha energy reading spiking!"

"Hard to starboard, down 36 degrees!" the captain called out.

There was a violent shudder to the *Seeker*, then the lights flickered briefly. Looking at my monitor, I saw that our port side defense field was almost non-existent.

"They near-missed us, captain," Forbes said, stating the obvious. "We've almost lost port side shields. Down to five percent"

"FTL drive is fluctuating," Lt. Grizik said. "We've got some overloaded paths and we're losing speed."

"Weapons status?"

"Portside point defenses are fluctuating. Main cannons and missile batteries are fully functional."

The captain was silent a moment, looking at her monitor, then she looked up with a steely expression in her face.

"Helm, set attack vector Gamma," she said. "Showing our fanny to this thing is only going to get our ass blown off."

Holy crap! We're going to go closer to that thing?

Chapter Twenty-Nine

To say I was sweating as I monitored all my weapon systems for functionality would be a vast understatement. The *Seeker* swung around on the tightest parabolic course we could manage, and Forbes, Kurakin and I coordinated with Solas in engineering to get port side defense batteries back to one hundred percent by robbing and rerouting power from other systems.

The time since this latest engagement began was fifteen minutes since the drone ships jumped. It felt to me like we'd been at it for an hour.

"Portside short guns won't go green. We've got about twenty percent power there," Forbes announced, obviously frustrated.

"We'll desperately need those if we get in close," Kurakin said.

"I can either work on that system, or I can try to get us full FTL speed again," Engineer Solas said from Forbes monitor. "My team is trying to get systems up all over the ship. If that's what happens with a 'near miss,' we'd better make damn sure that they don't get that monster beam anywhere close to us, much less a direct hit."

"Solas, we don't have the speed to outrun it anymore," the captain said. "So not only are we having that thing take pot shots at us, but it's getting closer and closer. We are now on an oblique attack vector. Prioritize weapon systems. Since we're heading toward them, we don't need the speed to run away."

Solas, whose image was on Forbes monitor, and I assume, the captain's, looked very surprised. "We're attacking, ma'am?"

"We're attacking. We can't dodge their attacks forever, so it's go time. I want weapons at full strength."

"Aye, Captain, prioritizing weapons."

"Helm, keep us in as close to a circle around that weapons platform as possible. When we get our systems working, we'll cut the circle and attack head on."

"Captain," Forbes said, "portside main cannon power is fluctuating now."

"Begging the captain's indulgence," Kurakin said, "but this Alpha module deflected our main cannon beams with little trouble last time. It obviously has a heavier magnetic defense system than its two sub-modules. We also haven't gotten close enough to know exactly what point defense weapons it has."

"Mr. Forbes, do you concur?"

Forbes looked at Kurakin for a moment, took a deep breath, and said, "I agree with the chief, Ma'am. Even if our weapon systems weren't acting up, it's still a toss-up as to whether we can punch through their shield system."

"Caught between the devil and the deep blue sea," Captain Yamashita said. "Your comments are noted, Chief, Commander, but we can't keep dodging forever."

"Then perhaps we should put our resources into the FTL drive, Captain," First Officer M'Buku said. "I hate showing them our heels, but if we could get full speed reinstated, we could not only outrun them, but the losses they've already suffered might convince them that pursuit is an unwise course, not worth the risk. Assuming an AI could make that decision."

The captain was silent a moment. "Mr. Solas, are you there?"

A moment passed then the chief engineer appeared on the monitor. "Solas here, Captain."

"Mr. Solas, can you give me a time estimate on repair of the FTL if we divert all resources there?" I knew that no captain likes to switch decisions, but Yamashita listened to her senior staff, not her ego.

"Captain, I believe we can get the engines back to full in approximately twenty-five minutes. It's a matter of replacing numerous shorted out relays and repairing the main equalizer."

"Can you make those repairs without our losing what speed and maneuverability we still have?"

"Affirmative. We just need to *not* get hit again."

"Time estimate on repairing all weapons systems, instead?"

Solas was silent for a moment. "It's difficult to be sure ma'am. We took a power surge through all those systems, and that has compromised many of the relays they depend on. Many of those are flickering from red to green, back to red. I'd guess maybe an hour and a half, two hours, to guarantee we won't have failures at inopportune times."

Captain Yamashita looked up at her first officer, face grim and replied to the chief engineer. "Mister Solas, I'm changing my original order. Get us full speed as fast as you possibly can, and we'll try to stay out of that terrible weapon's path."

"Aye aye, ma'am."

"Helm, keep us on a varied course, with random corrections. Science team, I want to know when that thing is getting ready to take another shot at us. This has turned into a vast game of chess, and being checkmated could happen all too easily."

Kolara had been replaced by a young lieutenant, and I felt the shift in gravitation as she began to fly "erratically." Kolara might've been a bit smoother in the transitions, but the lieutenant was certainly enthusiastic.

"Mister Voss, Ensign Dark Feather, you both started on the engineering tracks at the academy, did you not?" the captain asked.

"Aye, Captain." Dark Feather said. I nodded my affirmative.

"There's not a lot of gunnery required at this point, and I believe Commander Torvald can monitor our scanner and remoras without assistance for a while. He can warn us if the weapons platform is powering up to fire. I want you two to take a case of replacement power relays, and work solely on repairing the port side main cannon. If we do wind up in combat again, I want both of my main weapons functioning at one hundred percent."

Dark Feather and I were on our way to engineering a moment later. After we arrived, we found Commander Solas leading by example, his upper torso situated in a control panel. Tools and replacement parts lay scattered around him.

"Sir, the captain ordered Cadet Voss and I to work on replacing relays on the port main gun," Dark Feather said. "Can we have access to the supply lockers?"

Solas didn't even bring his head out from where he was working. He reached into the chest pocket of his coverall and pulled out his card, handing it to Dark Feather.

"Bring that back before you go to do your repairs, Ensign. I don't want any cards floating around, not after what happened in robotics."

"Aye sir," she replied. "Have it back to you in just a moment." Solas went back to his work without comment.

We pulled a case of replacement relays out, and I slung the plastic shoulder strap across my torso for easy carrying. Dark Feather returned the card, and we set out for the access panels for the port weapon systems.

"I hope we can get this sorted pretty quick," Dark Feather said.

"Yeah, me too. Without the mains, it'd be pretty damn hard to punch through that monster's defenses."

"That's not exactly what I meant, but yeah, that too."

"What did you mean?"

She looked at me, with a pained expression. "I just want this to be over. I want to be doing what we're meant to be doing, not fighting, exploring. And… I'm gonna be honest with you Tanner, I don't like feeling… afraid."

"I don't think anyone does, Ensign Dark Feather."

"Hey, when it's just us, you can call me Lilly. When we left space dock, it was so exciting, a grand adventure. I… want that feeling back."

"Yeah, I understand." And I did. I was not going to admit I'd been afraid from the moment we'd been first hit, but the truth was, it was a high-stress situation.

We rounded the corridor and found the hatch to the main access tunnel for the defense systems power grid.

"Okay," Dark Feather said. "Let's get this done as fast as possible."

A quick look at the section's main diagnostic board disabused of the notion that this was going to be easy. Flashing relays appeared all over the system.

"Oh, this is not good," I said. "There's at least sixty that are iffy, here. The way they're flickering from red to green, I wouldn't want to rely on any of these!"

"Look at this," Dark Feather said, "There are even some flickering on the starboard cannon, maybe fifteen or so. Tanner, I'm going to get those first, so we at least have one dependable main. You move to the other end of the hallway and start pulling the port side relays. When I finish with what I'm doing, I'll start on the port sides from this end of the hall."

"Meet in the middle?"

"Only if you're a slow poke. I'm spotting you fifteen starboard relays, and I bet I still get more done on the port side than you."

"Yeah, you keep dreamin', Lilly. Let's do this."

We separated, and I took a supply of new relays to the other end of the maintenance hallway. Once there, having transferred the diagnostic information to my Padd, I began the process of replacing the poorly performing and burnt out relays.

Done in small batches, it was a fairly quick job, but stacked in large groups, every step began to seem like it took an eternity. Unsnap the four latches covering the relay, pivot them out of the way, open the hatch, unsnap the four clips holding the relay in place, thumb the tab that would automatically slide the relay out at a glacial pace, pull the old relay, carefully set the new one in or it will slide back out, lock the pins, close the hatch, and secure it.

"We need a redesign here," I muttered under my breath. I felt a shift in my weight, and guessed that the lieutenant at the helm had just made another hard course change.

I was twenty relays in when Ensign Dark Feather showed up at the other end of the hallway for the port side relays.

"Starboard cannon relays are all good now," she said. "How are you doing over here?"

"I'm five ahead of you," I replied. "So, someone with the rank of ensign may be eating their words when it comes to being a slow poke. Just sayin'…"

"It ain't ovah 'til it's ovah, mister. Show me whatcha got."

I can't for sure say that the competition made us faster, but I'm pretty sure it did. Less than a half hour later, we were standing in front of the main diagnostic board again, and the news was good.

"Green boards all the way!" Dark Feather said. "We did it!"

"And in record time! And I only won by three relays so…" I noticed that she was looking at me funny. "Lilly?"

She didn't answer. She looked at me for another moment, reached out and grabbed my face and pulled me in for a kiss. To say I was surprised would be a gross understatement.

It was nice. *Real* nice. Warm, soft lips…

Suddenly, she pulled back, looking almost as shocked as I felt.

"I… uh…. I apologize, Cadet. That was totally inappropriate. I was, I guess caught up in the moment, the flush of success. I don't know what came over me."

"I… well… I wish you much success in the future, ma'am."

She looked away, face red. "We need to check with the bridge, now," she said, her voice all business. "Let's make sure that they read green on their boards also."

"Yes… yes, that would be good."

"Bridge," she said into the wall comm, "this is Dark Feather. We have replaced all the relays for the main cannons. Can you confirm your boards are green?"

"Affirmative, Ensign," Chief Kurakin's voice came from the comm. "The mains are go. We need for you to look at the point defense systems, too. Some of those are looking…"

She was cut off by Commander Torvald's voice. "Captain, they're getting ready to fire again."

"Evasive!" the captain said, and I felt the deck lurch beneath our feet from a quick turn.

The next thing I knew, I was flying though the air. I crashed into a bulkhead and a heavy weight smashed into me.

Darkness followed.

Chapter Thirty

"Tanner! Tanner! Can you hear me? Wake up!"

Oh… what the hell was that? Who is that?

"C'mon, Cadet! Don't die on me!"

"Lilly?"

"Yes, Tanner. Are you hurt?"

"I don't know. What happened?"

"I kinda landed on you. Other than that, I don't know, but I think we got hit again."

The lights were out, but the emergency lighting was enough to see that things were not going well. I got up, feeling a sharp pain in my ribs.

"You okay there, Tanner?"

"I think I might have some bad ribs. Hurts, but I can deal."

We looked down the corridor we had just been working on, and it wasn't a pretty sight. Smoke was leaking out of multiple points in the power feed and an automated fire suppression nozzle was spraying foam on a panel that had exploded outward. A few replacement relays weren't going to fix this.

The lights came on again, and a few moments later, the diagnostic computer came up with an intermittent fuzzing out. The readouts were not good. Starboard side weapons system showed numerous red spots on its power feed system. The port side systems were one large mass of flickering red.

"We're… defenseless," Dark Feather said. "All weapons systems are offline." She activated another tab for the defense fields. "Shields are offline too."

"Did we take a direct hit?" I asked.

"No, if we had, we wouldn't be having this conversation. But it was close enough to do a lot of damage. We are now completely defenseless."

"I hope Solas got those engines working. If not…."

"If not, we're screwed. And honestly…" she looked over at me. "If that's the case, I don't regret that stolen kiss.

"Yeah. Me neither."

"We should get to the bridge, see if we can do any good up there." she said.

We made our way through the corridors, in a few instances helping crew personnel get to their feet and on their way to the med center in the safe core. The increased damage to the defense system notwithstanding, at least this time we had light and gravity. This alone led me to believe Dark Feather was right, and we'd had another near miss, not a direct hit. I began to have hope that we were still moving forward under power, hopefully leaving our enemy behind.

I was proven wrong as soon as we reached the main bridge.

Looking at the view screens around the room, I could see by the stars passing across the monitors that we were no longer moving in a straight line. From the movement of the star field, I could see the ship was tumbling.

There was smoke in the air, but the life support system was pulling it into filtration vents. Several of the workstations were out, completely non-functional, and people were moving to the various exits, some of them injured. The captain was gone, and so was the first officer.

"Voss! Dark Feather!" Chief Kurakin came up to us, the side of her face bruised, and pointed toward the door we'd just come in. "Report to the Emergency Bridge. The main bridge is out of commission."

"Are things as bad as they seem, Chief?" Dark Feather asked.

Kurakin nodded. "It's bad. Report to the captain."

It took us longer than normal to make our way to the E-Bridge. People were making their way to the safe core and our route was crowded. That so many were moving to the protected interior of the ship wasn't a surprise, all one had to do was look out a port to see we were drifting.

"Ensign Dark Feather and Cadet Voss reporting, Captain," Dark Feather announced when we reached our destination.

"Take your stations," The captain said.

"For all the good it will do," I heard Commander Forbes say quietly. I quickly saw why. All the consoles in the secondary bridge were functioning perfectly, however the systems they were tied to were a mess. Red lights flickered across every diagram on the engineering station, though some were worse off than others.

"Captain, as best I can tell," Commander Torvald told her, "the enemy weapon determined our strategy and somehow changed the make-up of the last beam it sent toward us. There was a huge increase in electro-magnetic fields."

"But we're shielded against EMPs," the captain said.

"Not of this magnitude, though if we hadn't been so weakened by previous attacks, we might've weathered it better. Even if the engineers are able to work at three times the speed they've been working, even if we were able to enable the bots again, we couldn't get the ship moving again in less than a day."

They've been firing at us every seventeen and one-quarter minutes, Commander, the last shot was eleven minutes ago." Yamashita said.

"Yes ma'am. Scans from Remora 3 tell us that the enemy weapon is fifty percent recharged. We have no ability to maneuver." Torvald didn't say anything more, we all knew what he meant.

We're dead, we just don't know it yet.

The captain looked down at her hands for a moment, and when she looked up, I expected to see defeat in her eyes. It wasn't there.

"Mister Torvald, download logs and data collected to all four of the remoras and start R-1 and R-4 back toward the jump point we came in from. In the event we are destroyed, command all four probes to begin their mini jumps for Earth, via a secure and circuitous path."

"Aye Commander, downloading now."

"Make sure all records of this battle go also. I want the T.E.F. to know what we encountered here. Also, make sure that…"

"Beg pardon, Captain," Ensign Dark Feather interrupted.

Yamashita turned toward her looking mildly irritated. "What is it, Ensign?"

"Remora Two has left her tandem course with us… she's going toward the enemy gun platform."

"What? Torvald, are you doing this?"

"Negative, ma'am. I checked with the robotics department, and it's not them either."

"Is this some of Beltran's programming? Is the enemy weapons platform hacking our probes?"

I suddenly knew what was going on and my heart went into my throat.

"Remora Two has taken up a course paralleling the enemy, Captain," Dark Feather said.

"Looks like it did hack our Remora," the captain growled. "Just to add a little insult to injury."

"There is definitely data being shared…. But…"

"What is it, Mister Torvald?"

"Everything seems to be going from R-2 to the enemy, but nothing is being exchanged back as it would if our probe were being hacked." Torvald looked up at us all. "It's as if…"

"Captain!" Torvald cried out. "The enemy particle weapon…. it's powering down!"

"What?"

"Incoming message," the comm officer said. Her eyes widened. "Captain, it… it's from the enemy craft!"

"What!? What the hell? Put it on speaker!"

There was a moment of silence, then a very familiar voice emerged from the device.

"Well! That was a close one, wasn't it?"

Chapter Thirty-One

"Who is this?" the captain demanded. "To whom am I speaking? Are you offering us a chance to surrender?"

"Ah, no, actually, Captain Yamashita," the voice said. "I am formally offering this unholy terror as a subordinate vessel under your command. Which I guess makes you a commodore?"

"Who. Are. You."

"I am the Laldoralin AI designated Dora. I stowed away in Remora Two before the *Seeker* left Earth, coming from the *LV Kaialai*. I have been at loggerheads with the AI that controlled this drone since it first started getting cranky, and I have finally been victorious in that battle. I came along to make sure that my son, and of course the rest of you, survived the trip."

Captain Yamashita, no slouch in the uptake department, put two and two together almost instantaneously, and turned toward the one crew member who'd been intercepted on his way to join the *Seeker*. The rest of the bridge crew followed her lead and all turned to look at me. I could feel my face burning.

"Your son... I am assuming you are referring to our young Cadet Voss, over here."

"Yes, indeed. Tanner are you all right, sweetie?"

I choked. The captain looked at me, one eyebrow raised in a way that a junior officer would never want to have directed at them.

"Well? Answer your 'mother,' Cadet," she said with a cool tone.

It's hard to describe my relief at being alive coupled with the mortified embarrassment that made me want to die. It was as if the principles of Yin and Yang coalesced in my head and exploded.

"Hey, mom," I said. "I'm... I'm fine, we're pretty battered over here, though. Thanks for the save."

"You're most welcome, Tanner. Commodore, my scans indicate that the *Seeker* has lost propulsion, and I estimate your most basic repairs will take several days. This platform has magnetic traction capabilities that it uses to retrieve its subordinate modules, one of which I believe is salvageable. I am certain that the same magnetic field could be used to tow your vessel closer to the planet where there are numerous resources that could be mined from the moons encircling it. Should you so desire, of course."

"You said subordinate earlier, in regard to the platform you now inhabit, Dora. Does that mean you are applying to be part of the chain of command of my ship?" Yamashita said. "Will you comply with my orders?"

"As long as they are not self-destructive, Captain. I say that with respect, but I am a sentient being, and will not accept an order to destroy myself."

"Fair enough, though I am not in the habit of ordering execution for the crime of stowing away," Captain Yamashita said, a slight smile on her lips. "I will consult with my people, privately, and I would appreciate privacy while we mull over your offer. Are you still linked to Remora Two?"

"I am still existent in that frame also."

"I know what the scanning package on that probe can do, so I expect you to not scan us while we deliberate. Am I clear?"

"Crystal, Captain," Dora replied. "I am ceasing all scanning toward the *Seeker*, hail me when you wish to communicate again."

"Remora Two has ceased sending telemetry, Captain," Torvald said. "And it is now powering down."

"Commander Solas," the captain said into her chair mounted comm unit, "Please meet me in my office. We are off the hook for the moment. Commander M'Buku, Torvald and of course *you*, Mr. Voss, in my office."

I cannot remember a more uncomfortable meeting in my life.

"Mr. Voss, am I to understand that you knew about this... this... stowaway from the get-go?" the captain said. She didn't look happy.

"I found out just before we jumped, ma'am, just after the *Searcher* was destroyed."

"Young man, while I am deeply glad to still be here and not floating through space as atomized particles, I must tell you that I am somewhat disappointed in you. You have kept secrets from your superiors that are not small ones. The sort of secrets that could have you up on charges."

"Yes, Captain," I said, starting to feel that I was going to be joining Lisa Beltran in the brig for the rest of the journey. "I don't have a good excuse, other than Dora, as odd as it seems, was the only mother I ever knew, and I was afraid you would try to erase her."

"How does that work?" Torvald asked. "Having an AI as a mother, I mean."

"If you know my history, sir, I was born back in the mid-21st century. Both my mother and father were androids, very sophisticated ones. I didn't realize this until I was intercepted by the *Kaialai* and was told so by my sire just before we left."

"Let's not bring your famous father into this right now," the captain said.

"Ma'am, I didn't mean to…" Yamashita raised her hand to cut me off.

"Mr. Voss, I will decide what to do with you later. Right now, we have decisions to make. Gentlemen, we are still alive, something that I wouldn't have bet on twenty minutes ago. We are in a world of hurt, but we are alive," Captain Yamashita said, looking around the room. "I am putting it to you all, do we take Ms. Weapons Platform up on her offer? Mr. Solas? How bad off are we?"

"Not as bad as we could be, and certainly not as bad off if the AI hadn't involved herself," Solas said. "We've got blown out relays across the ship, so many that I think we'll use up a good portion of our stores just getting the FTL drive back online. That's with stealing from other lesser systems as well. Back at *Susanowo*, we have a vast amount of mineral and other resources, particularly on her second moon. We have mining craft and bots aboard and the replication printers to convert scavenged resources into everything we need without draining our own stores to the bone."

"I take it you're in favor, then? You trust this AI?"

"From an engineering standpoint, it only makes sense. As for trusting her? Since I am still breathing, I can confidently say that I'm a fan of said AI."

"Mr. M'Buku?"

"I have seen this young man do amazing things, and aside from the fact that he has saved our hides on no less than three occasions…"

"I am not disputing that, Commander," the captain said.

"This AI raised him, if I understand correctly. As far as I am concerned, that is reason to trust her. Why would she save us and have a sinister motive?"

"Den? Your thoughts?"

"Captain," Torvald said. "I don't have data to back this up, but my gut says we can trust her."

The captain stared at a small statue of the Buddha on her desk for a moment before looking up at Commander M'Buku, "Bosede, contact Dora, and tell her we will take her up on her kind offer. Oh, and take us out of battle stations, and inform the crew that we will be returning to the planet."

"Aye, Captain."

"Commander Solas, continue with repairs and start prepping for this grand resource accumulation. I assume that the jump drive is done for and that we'll need to send a Remora back to Earth to request rescue."

"No ma'am. We don't."

The captain stared at the chief engineer a moment. "Are you saying that we are in a salvageable situation, jump wise?"

"Captain, I believe with the resources we can harvest, and with the engineering team and equipment we have, we can realign the jump fins and get that reactor back online. We should at least make the attempt before we give up and cry for help."

"Time estimation?"

Solas shook his head. "It won't be easy, ma'am. I'm guessing months, possibly a year at the most. It is, of course, your call. One thing we will need to prioritize is getting the bots back in action. We need all of them, from largest to smallest to get this done."

The captain again looked at her statue for a time, pondering the issue.

"Gentlemen, I have never been a woman who likes failing. It appears that our science team are going to get a lot more time to study *Susanowo* than originally planned."

"Excellent!" said M'Buku.

"All right. You know your jobs, let's get this ship back in shape."

Chapter Thirty-Two

Things look better, now, a month later. Dora towed the *Seeker* into a high orbit around the planet that, with our remaining working thrusters, was sustainable.

The captain sentenced me to two weeks confinement to quarters for not informing her about Dora being aboard, to be served… someday, when every crew member isn't needed to get the ship back to one hundred percent.

I haven't been idle. First thing I was assigned was to rejoin the robotics staff in scrubbing and rebooting the float bots. Dora offered to scan the software packet that drove them to attack us, but the captain strongly refused. She said that the last thing we needed was for Dora to get infected with the homicidal software while in charge of a massive deadly weapon.

I think Mom was a bit insulted by that.

Two days after achieving orbit, the main FTL reactor was brought back on line, giving the ship full power again. The down side of this was that several overstressed systems then blew out. I think I mentioned that I, and everyone with any engineering training have not been idle. The plus for me was that I was assigned to work with Lilly Dark Feather.

The hull of the *Seeker* was a bit worse off than Solas had thought. The last shot from the weapons platform had actually rippled our hull in some places, causing micro-fractures. We will be here a while. Each damaged plate has to be removed, one at a time, recycled, replicated, and redeployed.

Crew morale is pretty good. That we only lost a few crew members is a minor miracle considering the battering we took, and everyone is cognizant of how close we came to losing it all. There is an air of optimism, stemming directly from Captain Yamashita's decision to continue our mission, and as predicted, the science teams are very happy to have so much time to study the planet.

The only unhappy spot is Lisa Beltran. She will spend the rest of this multi-year mission stuck in a fifteen by fifteen cell, only being able to leave for heavily guarded exercise periods. The guards are there as much to protect her as they are to keep her from mischief.

I go down and play chess with her twice a week, I guess chess not being a standard venue for us demon-spawn to steal the righteous person's soul. I'm simultaneously the one person on this ship she feels most compelled to kill, and also the closest thing to a friend she has.

Everyone is starting to also think ahead to the next system we're to explore, which long-range scans indicate may have a pair of habitable worlds.

Dora has been using the alien drone's repair system, which has an army of self-replicating repair robots, to make improvements to the alien vessel's jump drive, so we can take it with us. Onboard the newly christened *Musashi* (Captain's prerogative), Mom is also translating the computer system that the original owners used. Our science division is pretty excited to see what records we can assimilate and what new tech specs might be available.

My days are spent doing a couple hours studying in the morning of my shift, and then bouncing from one engineering task to another. Any hoopla from being an Acting Junior Tactical Officer is pretty much lost in tasks bent on fixing the ship, I haven't set foot on either bridge since we were towed here.

Honestly though, I find that these interesting times are actually pretty damn good, and I am lucky to be here.

Not bad for a guy who was tucked away in storage for a century and a half!

END.

AFTERWORD

A very long time ago, having read all the Doctor Seuss books in an elementary school library, a third grader decided it was time to move beyond "little kids" books. Telling the attentive librarian what he liked, she strolled across the room, picked out a book, and handed it to the little boy.

The book was Robert A. Heinlein's *Rocket Ship Galileo*, a more elegant story for a more civilized time. That led to *Starman Jones*, *The Door Into Summer*, *Glory Road*.

I was hooked for life.

I don't underestimate the influence these "juvenile" stories had on me. As an author, I can hear and feel these old stories bleeding into what goes on my own pages. As John D. MacDonald's Travis Mc-Gee books influence my *Mac Crow Thrillers*, Heinlein whispered over my shoulder to produce *Seeker One*.

I hope that you've enjoyed reading it as much as I did writing it.

I'd like to take a moment to thank my two editors. First, Anna Genoese for her diligent editing, both developmental and proof-reading. Any errors within now are most likely a case of the author being stubborn.

I'd also like to thank my wife Suzette Hollingsworth (an author of Victorian Sherlock Holmes mysteries) for giving me the unvarnished truth about sections of my books. Though this often results in my sulking for a few hours, her suggestions almost always improve my stories.

If you enjoyed this book, it would be very helpful if you could write a review, on Amazon or Goodreads. These reviews help me decide on whether a series is worth continuing, as well as giving the book more visibility on Amazon.com. The help would be very much appreciated.

-Clint Hollingsworth

Books by Clint Hollingsworth

The Mac Crow Thrillers
The Sage Wind Blows Cold
Death In The High Lonesome
The Deep Blue Crush

The Ghost Wind Chronicles
The Road Sharks

The Wandering Ones
(Graphic novels)
Book 1: The After Time
Book 2: The Mad Scout
Book 3: The Mission
Book 4: The Road Home
Scout Trail (Full color)
Nature Scout Emily (Comic/coloring book)

Other Graphic Novels
Tales of the Timewalker
Shin Kagé: Duel at the Derelict

Non-Fiction
Wolves in Street Clothing (With Kris Wilder)
Survival Knives (Tips for Choosing and Using)

Other NOVELS by Clint Hollingsworth

The Sage Wind Blows Cold

Deep in the woods, desperately following the trail, Mac comes upon an SAR volunteer face down in the forest with an arrow in his back. Little does MacKenzie Crow know, this is just the beginning of his problems.

Death in the High Lonesome

Mac and Rosa must escape from the deep mountains, with minimal gear during a blizzard, and to make things worse, they are being tracked by a killer who always seems to be three steps ahead of them. If Mac's skills of survival and tracking fail them, his and Rosa's bodies won't be found until spring time.

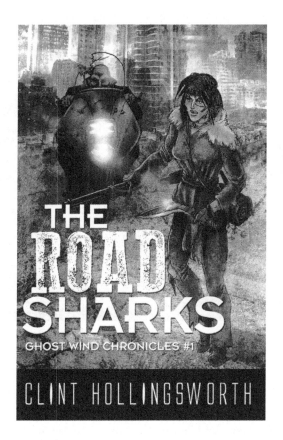

The Road Sharks (Ghost Wind Chronicles #1)

The story of Ravenwing's (The Wandering Ones) banished sister, **Ghost Wind.**

In 2057, warrior scout Ghost Wind finds herself banished from her people, cast adrift in a world ravaged by a man-made bio plague. Looking for a new home, she meets Eli, the handsome rider with many secrets, who hints at a place she might be welcome. Unfortunately, she also meets the vicious fusion cycle gang, the Road Sharks who do their best to make her life a living hell.

To survive, to have a new home, Ghost Wind realizes that she must be just as ruthless as her enemies, and that standing on the sidelines is a good way to lose everything.

Graphic NOVELS by Clint Hollingsworth
Available on Amazon

The Wandering Ones

2066 A.D.-The Pacific Northwest. A man-made plague has wiped out 80% of the world's population, dividing the survivors into the Clan of the Hawk (following the way of ancient Apache scout warriors, Ninjas and Trackers); the Western Alliance, a technology based society; and the Neo-Nazi Farnham's Empire.

It's been thirty years since the great Die-Off. Ravenwing, master scout of the Clan of the Hawk must take in three untrained apprentices from the technological Western Alliance, and teach them how to survive in the brutal post apocalyptic world of 2066 a.d.